Wedding Island

A romantic place in the Mediterranean weaves its magic!

La Isla Marina is hosting its first ever wedding and everything needs to be perfect! So estranged sisters Anna and Rosa are returning home to help their mother add the sparkle that the idyllic Mediterranean island deserves. But finding love was never meant to be on the agenda for either sister...until now!

As the island works its magic, the sisters find their way back to each other *and* the happily-ever-afters they never knew they deserved!

Find out more in

Baby Surprise for the Spanish Billionaire

One spontaneously romantic night with playboy Leo has surprising consequences...

Island Fling to Forever

Reunited with her old flame, Rosa discovers that second chances really are possible!

Both available now!

Dear Reader,

I love duets. I love writing them, and I love reading them—and working on Rosa and Jude's story gave me the best of both worlds! I got to write my own half of a duet *and* lose myself in the first book, *Baby Surprise for the Spanish Billionaire*.

My favorite thing about writing *Island Fling to Forever* had to be working with the very talented Jessica Gilmore to develop our characters, our island and our stories. Every time we brainstormed together, I ended the conversation wishing I could take a holiday to La Isla Marina to write the book!

It was so much fun to see my characters and the island we created through someone else's eyes—and writing. Rosa and her sister, Anna, might not always get along, but Jessica and I certainly did! So if you want to experience the events on La Isla Marina from another point of view, make sure you check out Anna and Leo's story, too. I adored it!

Most of all, I hope you enjoy your break away from the real world on our magical Spanish island as much as Jessica and I loved creating it.

Love and sunshine,

Sophie x

Island Fling to Forever

—

Sophie Pembroke

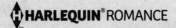

Recycling programs
for this product may
not exist in your area.

ISBN-13: 978-1-335-13507-0

Island Fling to Forever

First North American publication 2018

Copyright © 2018 by Sophie Pembroke

Printed in U.S.A.

Sophie Pembroke has been reading and writing romance ever since she read her first Harlequin novel at university, so getting to write them for a living is a dream come true! Sophie lives in a little Hertfordshire market town in the UK with her scientist husband and her incredibly imaginative six-year-old daughter. She writes stories about friends, family and falling in love—usually while drinking too much tea and eating homemade cakes. She also keeps a blog at sophiepembroke.com.

Books by Sophie Pembroke

Harlequin Romance

Wedding of the Year

Slow Dance with the Best Man
Proposal for the Wedding Planner

Summer Weddings

Falling for the Bridesmaid

The Unexpected Holiday Gift
Stranded with the Tycoon
Heiress on the Run
A Groom Worth Waiting For
His Very Convenient Bride
A Proposal Worth Millions
Newborn Under the Christmas Tree

Visit the Author Profile page
at Harlequin.com for more titles.

To Jessica,
for making this book twice as fun to write.

Praise for
Sophie Pembroke

"A poignant, feel-good and irresistible romantic treat that I struggled to put down, *Slow Dance with the Best Man* is a fantastic tale about second chances, healing from old wounds and finding the courage to fall in love that will touch the hearts of romance readers everywhere."

—*Goodreads*

CHAPTER ONE

ROSA GRAY TIED her dinghy up on the jetty and looked out across the water behind her, back towards the mainland. It would be so easy to just hop back in the boat and set sail again for mainland Spain. And, actually, it was entirely possible that no one would even miss her. Especially her sister, Anna.

Except that her mother had sounded panicked when she called. Sancia Garcia never panicked. Not when she decided to leave her husband when Rosa was sixteen, not when Rosa's grandfather died three years ago and left Sancia in sole charge of the luxury island resort of La Isla Marina. Not even when Rosa was eight and had tried a flying dive off the highest point of the island coastline, and almost brained herself on the rocks below.

No, Rosa's mama was the epitome of laid-back grace. Of letting things work themselves out in time, and trusting the universe to provide.

Until, it seemed, she was faced with the wedding of a New York socialite, and the realisation that the luxury island resort was no longer quite so luxurious.

Rosa stared up the wide, open path that led to the main villa at the centre of the island. Dotted on either side were a few of the low, white bungalows that made up the island's accommodation, all shining bright in the fading afternoon sun.

It still looked pretty good to her. But then, maybe she had a slightly skewed view of luxury, after a month spent deep in a South American jungle for a job. Or, more likely, St Anna had already fixed whatever she believed was wrong with La Isla Marina.

Anna always believed she could fix anything, if she just made enough lists, worked hard enough, or nagged often enough. But she hadn't been able to fix their family, had she? Rosa was almost hoping she'd given up trying by now. If she'd learned anything from her mother it was that, at a certain point, the only thing to do was to cut and run. No point flogging a dead horse and all that.

Or, in Rosa's case, no point dreaming that her family would ever be the sort of Christmas-advert perfect family where everyone was equally respected and listened to. So why hang around and wait for the impossible?

Which didn't explain why she was on the damn island in the first place. The only thing Rosa could put that down to was that thin thread, the one that started deep down inside her, connecting her to her mother, her sister, even her father. The one she'd never been able to sever, no matter how far or how fast she ran.

Maybe Anna felt the same. Why else would Rosa's big sister be here fixing everything for the mother who'd run off and left her in charge when she was only eighteen? Unless it was just to prove she could.

Either way, Rosa was about to find out.

Shouldering her rucksack, Rosa set off for the central villa at a steady pace. No point putting it off now she was here: it was time for the grand family reunion.

La Isla Marina was less than a mile across, so it didn't take her very long to reach the villa that housed the family and staff accommodation, as well as the administrative offices for the island. On the way, Rosa searched for changes that had taken place since she was last there, for her grandfather's funeral, three years ago. Surely there must be some? But she was hard pressed to find them.

Pausing on the path, Rosa drank in the view

of the central villa, surrounded by lush greenery and bright flowers. The large white building, with its graceful arches and turrets, and tiled courtyards within, looked more like a Moorish palace than a Spanish villa, but to Rosa it had always felt like home in a way that nowhere else in the world did. Its twin turrets, housing two bedrooms—one for her and one for Anna—had seemed like the most magical places ever, when she was small. In some ways they still did.

How strange to be back again, without her grandparents there to welcome her home. Three years since her *abuelo* had died, and another year before that without her grandmother, and Rosa knew that she'd never grow used to it. It was almost as if the soul had left the island when theirs had.

Another reason she hadn't made it back for so long.

Her fingers itched for her camera, packed safely in her bag, to capture this perfect moment—the villa almost glowing in the sunshine, the azure sky behind it—before any people intruded on the picture and the calm was broken.

She wondered what sort of a welcome *would* be waiting for her. Sancia would be pleased to see her, as always. Rosa was her baby girl, and for ever would be. She might not be the academic success her sister was, or be the useful, sensible sort of daughter that parents wanted, but Rosa knew her mother would always adore her all the same. And, unlike her father, respect her life choices, which meant a lot.

Of course, it was probably easier for Sancia to let Rosa be Rosa from afar, wasn't it? When she only saw her for holidays and high days, even before she left to explore the world, as soon as she turned eighteen? That was what Anna would say, anyway. Anna who had taken over to deal with Rosa's 'difficult teenage years', as their father referred to them.

She needed to stop channelling Anna's thoughts, or she was going to drive herself mad. Except Sancia wasn't the only family member waiting on the island. She might have called Rosa for help, but Rosa knew she wasn't Sancia's first call. That had gone to Anna, the useful, sensible daughter. As always.

And St Anna wouldn't have made their mother wait two weeks, as Rosa had. Whatever their differences—and there were plenty— Anna would have dropped everything to help Sancia. In her defence, Rosa had been stuck in the middle of a South American rainforest at the time, and contractually bound to stay there until she had the full story and photos she needed for the magazine hiring her. But that didn't mean that Anna wouldn't have something to say about that delay. Or, knowing her sister, many some-things.

And nothing at all to say about Rosa's career successes. Anna probably didn't even know that Rosa was booked up months in advance, when she wanted to be, by publications looking for her particular style of photo journalism. Rosa was making quite a name for herself in her in-dustry, not that it would mean anything to Anna and their father. Anything that happened outside the dreaming spires of Oxford's academic elite simply didn't matter to either of them.

Oh, well. La Isla Marina might not be huge, in island terms, but it had plenty of hidden cor-ners and secret places—and Rosa had discov-ered all of them over the years. From secret coves for skinny-dipping to secluded bars and 'relaxation zones' dotted between the bunga-lows, Rosa could always disappear when she needed to. And if the worst came to the worst, she could pick up one of the island's boats and head across to the mainland and Cala del Mar for some truly excellent tapas and views.

And she didn't have to stay long. She never did. Her *modus operandi* was get in, get what she needed, and move on again. Always had been. It served her well in her work, and she had a feeling it would serve her just as well on La Isla Marina this week. She loved her mother dearly, but it was generally better for everyone if they didn't spend more than a couple of weeks in each other's company. They were just too alike—in the same way that she and Anna were just too different—to get along all the time.

It was all about identifying objectives. On assignments, she knew which shots she needed to tell the story that was playing out before her. Here, it was about reassuring her mother, making sure that everything was stable on the island again, then moving on guilt free.

Chances were, Anna would already have done all the hard work for her, and Rosa could be on her way again inside the week. There was a situation in Russia that she'd been keen to get closer to...

A pang of guilt twanged through her as she thought about her sister. How bad had things on the island really had to get for Sancia to call *her*? And how mad would Anna be that Rosa had left her to deal with it?

The thing was, it wouldn't have mattered if Rosa had taken the first flight out. Anna, based over in Oxford, would still have beaten her there by sheer virtue of time zones and air miles. Which meant that Anna would have already taken charge, and taken over the island.

Anna had always made it very clear that she expected to do everything herself, her way, and to feel martyred about it afterwards. So really, what point had there been in rushing?

Besides, it wasn't as if Sancia had dragged Anna away from anything important. Probably. Last time they'd spoken, Anna had been busy living up to their father's academic ideals, and giving up any semblance of fun or a social life to mother him excessively in Sancia's absence—despite the fact Professor Ernest Gray was an intelligent, grown man who could clearly take care of himself.

Rosa couldn't really imagine that that situation might have changed in the last three years.

Three years. Had it really been three years since she last spoke to Anna? Three years since their grandfather died? Three years since she'd yelled back a whole host of home truths at her sister, then left the country? Three years since she'd been back in England, or to La Isla Marina? Three years since…well. She wasn't thinking about that. About him.

She'd made a point of not thinking about Jude Alexander for a grand total of thirty-six months. She wasn't breaking that streak now.

It was just that it was all tied up together in her head. That awful argument with Anna, everything that happened with Jude, why she had to get out of the country…and now, knowing she was about to see Anna again had brought it all back.

Well, tough. She was going to rock up to the villa, deal with her sister, hug her mother, accept the inevitable offer of a glass of wine, check that everything was fine now, and make plans for leaving again.

Easy.

Hopefully.

With a sigh, Rosa shifted her bag higher on her shoulder and carried on walking. She'd already lingered on the side of the path longer than necessary. The last thing she wanted was one of the guests reporting some suspicious character with a bag loitering in the greenery.

She frowned. Actually, she hadn't seen any guests. At all.

It was late May; the island should be teeming with holidaymakers, enjoying all the luxuries the resort had to offer. So where was everyone?

Unless things were worse than she thought…

Rosa quickened her step and, in a brief few minutes, found herself standing in the cool, tiled reception area of the central villa. White arches soared overhead, leading to small, secluded balconies with wrought-iron bars and plenty of brightly coloured cushions on their chairs. Just beyond the main area, through wide open doors, was the central courtyard, with reflecting pool and more lush potted greenery, and plenty of places to sit and take in the view. In high season, it was used as the main restaurant area for breakfasts, and even now it should be buzzing with early evening cocktail seekers.

It was empty. As was the reception desk.

Refusing to ring a bell in her own home, Rosa dropped her bags by the desk, bypassed the winding staircase to the upper levels, and the hidden doorway that led to the private, family quarters. Instead, she moved through the courtyard, and out the other side of the villa onto the sheltered patio that overlooked the beaches and the wide expanse of turquoise sea on the more exposed side of the island.

There, at last, she found signs of life, and her family. If not exactly the ones she'd been expecting.

She froze, her chest tightening, as if she were preparing to run—or hide. Surely her eyes were playing tricks on her?

'Dad?' Rosa pulled her sunglasses off to be absolutely sure of what she was seeing. Nope, she hadn't imagined it. There, looking incongruous in a white shirt and stone-coloured jacket over chinos, and a panama-style hat, sat Professor Ernest Gray himself, a thousand miles and more away from where Rosa had expected him to be, locked up in the ivory towers at Oxford.

Of course, he was playing Scrabble with a dark-haired guy who had his back to her, so he was still finding some way to demonstrate his mental prowess. As usual. Rosa pitied his opponent.

Except now she'd drawn his attention, she'd given him a new target. It could only be a matter of time now before he turned his sharp mind and sharper words onto her—her choice of career, her lack of education, her inability to stay in one place, her unreliability... How could he possibly get through all her faults in one short visit?

'Rosa.' Her father inclined his head towards her, without smiling. 'Your mother told us you'd be joining us. Eventually.'

And that was about all the family love and welcome she could expect from him, Rosa supposed. What was he even doing here? As far as she knew, he'd had as little contact with Sancia as possible, after she left, and they'd been separated ten years or more now. In all that time he'd *certainly* never visited the island that she'd escaped to. Why would he? Following Sancia to La Isla Marina would have been tantamount to admitting that he'd made a mistake, given her reasons to leave him. And if Rosa understood one thing about her father it was that Professor Ernest Gray would *never* admit that he was wrong.

So what could have brought him here now? Were things worse than she thought? Maybe it wasn't the island that had Sancia panicked. Maybe it was something else. She should have got here sooner…

Her heart raced as all the worst-case scenarios flooded her mind. Rosa grabbed for the memory of meditation practice in India, two years ago, and focussed on her breath until she had it under control again.

No point getting worked up until she had some answers. Which meant asking questions. 'Where is Mama? And Anna? And the guests, come to that? I was expecting—'

She didn't get any further, because as she started talking her father's Scrabble companion turned around and Rosa got a good look at his face, pale and shadowed in the cool of the patio shade but still absurdly perfect, with cheekbones that emphasised the beautiful shape of his face, and the incredible blue of his eyes.

It was too late to run. Too late to hide. And Rosa didn't even know *how* to fight this sudden intrusion. Her whole body seemed fixed to the spot as a hundred perfect memories ran through her mind, racing over each other, all featuring the man in front of her.

Whatever she'd been expecting from her return to La Isla Marina faded away. Because there in front of her, on her Mama's back patio, sat the last person she'd ever expected to see again—and a perfect reason to join Sancia and start panicking.

Jude Alexander.

La Isla Marina, Jude had decided within a few hours of his arrival, was the perfect hideaway from the real world. It had sun, sand, sangria and—most importantly for him—solitude. In fact, he wasn't all that bothered about any of the first three items on the list, as long as he was left alone while he was there.

Fame, it turned out, was overrated. Especially the sort of fame that meant he couldn't go anywhere without being recognised, or do anything without the world having an opinion about his actions. It might have taken him a while to see the downsides of celebrity, but now that he had…well, Jude was experiencing them in spades.

So it was sort of ideal that his main companion on the island was an ageing Oxford professor who hadn't got the slightest idea who Jude was. Professor Gray was perfectly content to play Scrabble for hours, or talk about events of the last century, or the one before—without ever asking a question about Jude's own life. The man's self-absorption—or perhaps his preoccupation with the historical world—made Jude's quest to escape the person he'd become all the easier. The professor hadn't even explained why he was there himself, let alone asked Jude what had brought him to the remote Spanish island.

If Professor Gray didn't know or care who Jude was, his ex-wife, Sancia, and daughter Anna were too busy to even notice. Apparently there was some sort of event happening at the island later in the month—Sancia hadn't gone into details—and it was all hands on deck to prepare for it. All hands except his and Professor Gray's. Jude got the feeling he'd been cast in the role of companion, or perhaps nurse, to the professor since they'd arrived together. Whatever the reason, it was all working out fine for him.

Until a voice he'd never dreamed or hoped he'd hear again spoke.

'Dad?' He hadn't realised what he was hearing, at first. That one word wasn't enough to make the memories hit—which surprised him, given how many other things seemed to trigger them.

'Rosa.' That name, spoken in Professor Gray's cultured tones. That was his first clue. 'Your mother told us you'd be joining us. Eventually.'

But still, Rosa had to be a reasonably common Spanish name, right? There was no reason to imagine it was *his* Rosa. Or, rather, the Rosa who'd made it very clear that she'd rather leave the country than belong to him.

The Rosa he'd known, three years before, was probably still thousands of miles away on the other side of the world, chasing whatever dreams he couldn't be a part of. Dreams she'd never even told him about, even as he'd spilled every one of his to her.

That Rosa couldn't be here. That was insane. Maybe the latest events in New York had actually driven him mad after all. It would explain the midnight flight to Spain, anyway.

'Where is Mama? And Anna? And the guests, come to that?' But as she spoke Jude realised there was no point denying what he was hearing, not any more. Only one person, one voice, had ever made his heart shudder like that.

There was no point hiding. La Isla Marina was his best shot at a hiding place, and she was already here.

Time to face his demons.

Jude turned around.

'I was expecting—' Rosa cut herself off, staring. 'Oh.'

She looked just the same—same wild dark hair, same wide, chocolate eyes with endless lashes. Same sweet, soft mouth. Same curves under her jeans and T-shirt, same smooth skin showing on her bare arms. Same neat, small feet shoved into flip-flops.

Same woman he'd fallen in love with, last time they met.

'Hello, Rosa.' Jude tried for a smile—that same smile that graced album covers and posters and photo shoots. The one that never felt quite real, any more. Not since Rosa left. And definitely not since Gareth.

There was no answering smile on Rosa's face though, only shock. Who could blame her? It wasn't as if he'd planned this, either.

He might have done, three years ago, if he'd known about this place—or rather, known that this was her home. Because now, too late, all the pieces were falling into place. She'd left him to go back to her mother's family home, for her grandfather's funeral—and never come back again. La Isla Marina must have been where she'd run to.

If he'd known that then, would he have followed?

Or would he have accepted that she'd not told him where she was going for a reason?

Oh, who was he kidding? Even if he'd known where she was, he'd have sat there waiting for her to come back because he'd had *faith* in her.

Something that had turned out to be seriously misplaced. And the day he'd realised that was the terrible day that everything had happened with Gareth, and he wasn't going anywhere for a while. Except down, in a despair spiral he almost hadn't made it out of. And then, suddenly, up the charts, for all the wrong reasons.

After Gareth, how could he have let himself see her again, anyway? He'd broken every promise he'd ever made for this woman, and she'd walked out anyway, leaving his world destroyed and empty.

Of course he hadn't chased her across the globe. Even if he'd wanted to, and hated himself for that.

So many conflicting emotions tied up in the curvy, petite woman standing in front of him, all tangled and tight around his heart. Would he ever escape those bonds?

Rosa was still staring at him, stunned, and Jude hunted around for something to say. For some of the many, many words he'd wished he could say to her over the last few years. The accusations, the questions, the declarations, anything. But nothing came out.

'You two know each other?' Professor Gray was looking between them, confused.

Something about his voice seemed to snap Rosa out of her shock, as she gave them both a lopsided smile that never quite reached her eyes. 'Oh, Dad, everyone knows Jude Alexander. He has possibly the most recognisable face in the world, right now.'

Professor Gray turned his curious gaze onto Jude, as if searching for fame in his features.

'Your daughter photographed me for a publication a few years ago,' he explained, blandly. No hint of the true story between that four-week study when Rosa travelled with them on tour, capturing every moment of their rise to fame. Of Gareth's last tour. 'I'm in a band, you see.'

'*A* band?' Rosa scoffed. 'Jude is the frontman of The Swifts, Dad. Hottest band of the decade, some are saying.' She raised an eyebrow at him, and Jude tried not to squirm under it. Not just because of the inevitable uncomfortableness that always came when someone referred to *him* as the frontman, instead of Gareth. But because he had *so* been enjoying not being *that* Jude Alexander for a while.

'You know I don't follow popular culture, Rosa.' Professor Gray dismissed his daughter's words with a wave of his hand. 'But Jude here is an almost competent Scrabble player, at least.'

Jude watched as Rosa's gaze flicked over to him at her father's words, meeting his for just a second. Just long enough for him to feel the same connection he'd experienced the night they'd met. It hit him deep, inside those tangled threads around his heart, a piercing guilt tied up with want and need and lust.

Still. Nice to know he hadn't imagined it, that connection. Even if it clearly never had the same effect on Rosa as it had on him.

'I'm so glad you've found a playmate, Father,' Rosa said, her tone scathing. 'But Jude's Scrabble abilities don't answer any of my questions. Where are Mama and Anna? And what on earth are you doing here?' She glanced at Jude again as she asked the last question, leaving him uncertain as to whose presence she was most baffled by.

Jude didn't blame her.

Now the initial shock of her arrival had passed, he found himself watching her more closely, looking beyond the familiarity of the woman he'd known so intimately—if, apparently, incompletely—three years ago. There *were* changes, ones he hadn't initially spotted. She was leaner now, he realised, harder even. Her mass of long, dark curls had been tamed back into a braid that hung over her left shoulder, and her dark eyes were far more wary than he remembered. Even in her relaxed jeans and fitted T-shirt, her sunglasses dangling loosely from her fingers, she looked poised to run at any moment. As if this beautiful island resort was more of a trap than her home.

What had made her look that way? And why, after all this time, did he even care?

'Your mother is talking with the cook about dinner, I believe,' Professor Gray said. 'And as for your sister, I have no idea.'

'She went to Barcelona with Leo,' Jude put in, since apparently he was paying more attention to the professor's family than he was.

'Leo?' Rosa's nose crinkled up as she said the name. 'Who on earth is…? Never mind. Dad, why are you here?'

Professor Gray observed his daughter mildly. 'Why, is it such a crime for a man to wish to spend time with his family?'

From the look Rosa gave him in return, Jude rather thought her answer might be yes.

'Professor Gray?' Maria, the only non-family member of staff that Jude had actually met on the island, appeared in the villa doorway. 'There is a phone call for you at Reception? From Oxford?'

'Still no mobile phone, huh, Dad?' Rosa asked.

'I have one,' Professor Gray answered, loftily, as he got to his feet. 'I merely do not see the requirement for it to always be on my person. Or switched on.'

'Of course you don't.'

As Professor Gray made his way into the villa, Jude found himself staring at Rosa again. What was it about this woman that captivated him so, that he couldn't look away, even now, after everything that had happened because he'd fallen for her? He wished he knew. Maybe then he could break free of it. As it was…

'So.' Rosa moved to take her father's chair opposite him, and Jude knew exactly what was coming next.

She was going to ask him a question, and he was going to have to decide how much of the truth he wanted to tell her. Given that last time he'd told her everything—opened up every part of himself and shared it with her—and she'd left anyway, he had a feeling that this time discretion might really be the better part of valour.

Or, as Gareth would have said, if he were still alive to say it, *Screw me once, shame on you. Screw me twice…*

Jude wasn't going to let that happen. In any sense of the word.

Rosa sat down, and caught his eye across the table.

'What are you doing here, Jude?'

Jude opened his mouth, and prepared to lie.

CHAPTER TWO

HE WAS GOING to lie to her.

Three years, and Rosa could still see the tell in the way Jude glanced to the side before speaking.

She supposed she couldn't blame him. She hadn't exactly done much to earn the truth from him.

But on the other hand, this was her home, her place—and she'd never told him about it. Had he been stalking her, searching for her, these last three years? Had he come here to find her? And if so, why on earth now, not three years ago?

No, that was ridiculous. She hadn't known she was coming herself until two weeks ago, and she had a hard time believing that Sancia and Anna had teamed up to come up with some outrageous story to get her there, just to help Jude out.

Unlikely as it seemed, this had to be some kind of crazy coincidence.

Rosa wasn't entirely sure if that made it better or worse.

'Believe it or not, I came here to work on some new music,' Jude said. Just the words conjured up memories of watching him composing, trying out new melodies on his guitar at the back of the tour bus, folded up to sit on the narrow bunk she lay in. Some of the most precious moments they'd spent together in that too-short month were times like that, when no one else was there or awake, when it was just them and the music.

But she couldn't think about that now. Memories weren't going to help her figure out what the hell was going on here.

'So you had no idea that this was my mother's family home?' Rosa asked, her eyes narrowing. It didn't hurt to double check these things, right?

'None at all.' That, at least, seemed to be the truth. So where was the lie? He was a musician, of course he'd come here to work on music. Except where was the rest of the band, in that case? Or what was left of it.

The memory hit her harder than she'd expected. An article online she'd caught by chance, that had left her crying in a foreign airport for a man she'd known and grown fond of. For another star gone too soon. And for Jude, left behind—the only time she'd let herself cry for him at all.

The band she'd known, when she'd toured with Jude that summer, wasn't the same band he was with now. Not without Gareth.

No wonder he hadn't come after her. He'd been dealing with his own tragedy, while she'd left to attend her *abuelo*'s funeral and had her whole world changed.

But that didn't change the truth of him being here, now. 'So you expect me to believe that this is just a bizarre and unfortunate coincidence?'

'If you like.' Jude gave a small, one-sided shrug, but the smile on his lips told her that wasn't entirely how he'd put it. 'To be honest, it doesn't much matter to me what you believe, any more.'

It had once, though. For one brief, shining month in time, what Rosa had believed had mattered to Jude Alexander. And what he'd believed about her had mattered to her, too.

Which had only made it harder to let him down when she'd walked away.

Of course, that was how she knew it was the right decision, too. But that didn't mean there hadn't been moments since, days when she'd been lost and alone and confused, when she'd wondered how different things would be if she'd gone back to him when she'd left La Isla Marina, instead of hightailing it for the Middle East, then Australia, then the Americas.

A whole life she'd thrown away and never lived. Of course she thought about it. She just didn't let herself imagine it too often, or in too much detail. She didn't want the regrets—not when she'd done the right thing, and found the life she'd always promised herself because of it.

She wondered if Jude would understand that, if she told him. Or maybe he'd been relieved when she hadn't come back. After all, he'd chased and caught his own dreams, too. But they'd come at a high price.

Rosa picked up a few of her father's Scrabble tiles, and began rearranging them on the rack, spelling out Spanish words he'd never use, for her own amusement, trying to find the words she needed to say.

In the end, she settled for blunt. It was her style, after all.

'I heard about Gareth. I'm sorry. You know how fond I was of him.' It had been hard not to adore Gareth. His optimism, his openness, the joy he'd found in the world... It was hard to imagine the band without him.

Hard to imagine Jude without his best friend.

Jude looked away. 'Yeah.' The curt word told Rosa her sympathies weren't enough. Of course they weren't.

Nothing could make up for Gareth's death. Certainly not anything *she* had to offer.

It wasn't her place to ask what happened, to tell Jude he could talk to her, if he needed to. Wasn't her place to comfort him for a three-year-old tragedy that obviously still cut him deep.

She'd given up that place when she left.

Time to move on. She was never good at the touchy-feely stuff, anyway.

'So, where are the others?' Always a good way of figuring out whether a person was lying to her—ask a question she already knew the answer to. 'Jimmy and Lee and Tanya?' The rest of The Swifts. After all, Jude hadn't got this famous all on his own, whatever the gossip magazines seemed to think.

And right now, the gossip sites didn't seem to know *what* to think. Rosa didn't make a point of following Jude's every career move, or anything—in fact, she made a point of not listening to his music any more than she had to, which was made more difficult by the fact it seemed to be playing *everywhere* at the moment. Even in the rainforest, someone had brought speakers and been playing The Swifts when they'd set up camp the other week.

But even she hadn't been able to avoid the news that Jude Alexander had dropped off the face of the earth. The rest of the band had been photographed out and about in New York City, but there had been no sign of their lead singer.

Not that Rosa had been concerned about that. Much.

'New York, I think.' Jude looked away again, down at his own tiles. He wasn't lying, so maybe just hiding something? Rosa couldn't tell, any more. 'I'm working on some…different stuff.'

'Solo stuff?' Because *that* she hadn't read anywhere online. 'You're planning on leaving The Swifts?'

'No,' Jude said, too quickly. 'I'm not. I couldn't. I just… I needed some time away, is all.'

'And you picked La Isla Marina?' Because, really, that was too much of a coincidence to not bear some investigation.

'I heard someone talk about this place once. I can't remember who, exactly. One of Sylvie's friends, maybe.'

Sylvie. That would be Sylvie Rockwell-Smythe, Rosa's ever-helpful brain for useless knowledge filled in. Jude's beautiful, red-headed, heiress and model girlfriend. Exactly the sort of woman a celebrity like Jude should be dating.

Except, if he was here in paradise, and she was still in New York… 'How is Sylvie?'

'We split up,' Jude said, shortly.

'Ah. Sorry.' There was that old talent for putting her foot in it, rearing up again. One day she'd learn not to just say the first thing that popped into her head. Maybe.

Jude shrugged. 'I wouldn't be.'

'Like that, huh?'

'Pretty much.'

Rosa sat back and surveyed him, taking in the changes the last three years had wrought on a face she'd known so well, once. He looked thinner. No, not thinner, exactly. Leaner. As if some stylist had decided to play up his pale and interesting aspect. But they couldn't style away Jude's broad shoulders, or the muscles in those arms.

But he looked tired. Worn down, maybe.

'So. How's fame going?'

'Overrated.' Jude met her eyes. 'Haven't you heard the latest? The entire of the continental US is talking about it.'

'I've been kind of out of touch,' Rosa admitted. 'I was working on a story down in South America…wait.' Hadn't she read something about a book, somewhere? A kiss-and-tell sort of a book, all about Jude? Maybe Sylvie had something to do with that… 'Is this about the book?'

'Jude: The Naked Truth.' Jude shook his

head in disgust as he quoted the title. 'That's the one.'

Whoever had written it should have come and found Rosa. She could have told them plenty of secrets about Jude Alexander.

She wouldn't have, of course. That was just one of the many differences between her and Sylvie. That and the fact that the other woman was a supermodel. And at five feet three and with too many curves, Rosa would definitely never be that.

'I haven't read it.'

Jude didn't respond, and Rosa resigned herself to looking him up on the internet once she'd got her laptop hooked up to the island Wi-Fi. It wouldn't be the first time, anyway. And Jude didn't have many secrets from the media these days, it seemed to Rosa. She could probably download the eBook and know everything she wanted to about him in a couple of hours of reading.

Except she didn't want to. Those books never told the whole truth, anyway. And she knew more about him than any pages could contain.

Or she had. Once.

Before.

She turned back to her father's Scrabble tiles, and ignored the letters 's' 'e' and 'x' to find something else to think about.

'So. Been a while,' Jude said, and Rosa looked up from her Scrabble tiles to take in the sight of him in the sunshine again.

He was too pale, she decided. He couldn't have been on the island long or he'd have lost that grey pallor that came from too long spent inside with only his guitar for company.

But he was still every bit as gorgeous as she remembered. As she'd tried to forget.

Her fingers flexed, reaching for the camera that wasn't hanging around her neck for once. She wanted to capture him here, now, in the moment. A comparison piece to the famous, laughing photo of him she'd taken three years ago. One photo in thousands she'd taken that month, but the one everyone remembered most. The one that had made her name. Kick-started her career, when The Swifts had hit the big time.

She'd been assigned to the up-and-coming band by a magazine she'd done some work for before, asked to follow them on tour for an indepth photo piece with some interviews. Someone high up at the magazine had a feeling about them, she'd been told, and they wanted to get in there first, before anyone else.

Whoever that person was, they'd been right. And they'd changed Rosa's world with that one commission, in too many ways to count.

If she hadn't taken the job, she'd never have

taken the photo that started her rise to the top of her profession, that gave her the luxury of picking and choosing jobs wherever she wanted in the world.

If she hadn't taken the job, she'd never have met Jude. And if she hadn't met Jude, she wouldn't have spent three years taking any job that kept her away from England, Spain and New York.

'Three years.' As if he didn't already know.

'You look good.'

'You look pale.'

Jude laughed, the first true emotion she'd seen from him since she arrived. 'You never were very good for my ego, were you?'

'You never needed me for that.' He'd always had plenty of hangers-on and groupies, ready to tell him how wonderful he was, even back then, before The Swifts took over the music world. Gareth might have been the lead singer, but Jude was the mysterious lead guitarist, and that had its own appeal.

And he'd had Gareth to keep him optimistic. To keep him humble.

How had he coped without him?

She should have called. It was three years too late to be asking these questions. But back then…she couldn't.

Rosa shoved the last of the Scrabble tiles

aside and got to her feet. 'I really should go
and find my mother. Let her know I'm here.'

Jude inclined his head in a small nod. 'Of
course.'

She waited, just a moment, in case he was
going to say anything more, but he was already
studying his letters again. If those groupies could
see him now—wild-child rock-and-roll star plays
Scrabble. Wouldn't they be disappointed?

Was *she*, though? Rosa wasn't even sure. Already this trip home was nothing like she'd expected.

But she couldn't be certain if that was a bad
thing or not. Not yet.

She paused as she reached the archway leading into the villa.

'Jude?'

He looked up. 'Yeah?'

'Did you really not know I'd be here?'

'Honestly?' Jude gave her a sardonic smile.
'I would never have come if I did.'

Rosa looked away. Well. That told her.

And really, what else was she hoping for?

Shaking away the conversation with Jude,
Rosa headed inside to find her mother. And
some answers.

Jude watched Rosa go, then realised she'd
stopped, just inside the archway to the villa.

Not that he cared.

He shouldn't care.

He absolutely shouldn't care enough to want to watch her every move.

Except…he did. Even after everything.

Trying not to be obvious about it, Jude tilted his chair just enough for him to see inside the villa, to where Rosa had found her mother. Both women seemed far too preoccupied with each other to be worrying about him, so he took advantage of their distraction to shift his chair around a bit more, so he could watch them properly.

It wasn't his place to spy on a reunion, he knew. But since his own with Rosa had been so anticlimactic, he wanted to know what a real one would look like.

Inside, Sancia threw her arms around Rosa and held her tight, swaying her back and forth with her outpouring of affection.

Once, Jude had imagined that his and Rosa's reunion might be full of love, like that. Filled with passion, at least—the same kind of passion they'd shown each other during their brief time together.

Sometimes, late at night, he'd allowed himself to picture it. Rosa coming back, finding him backstage, just as he was finishing a gig. He'd be on a performance high, anyway, and when he saw her…everything would crystallise, fall into place. He'd sweep her up into his arms and never let her go again.

Except she'd never come back, had she?

And then Gareth had died, and he'd been so lost. So hopeless, without his best friend. He'd needed Rosa, then.

But she was long gone. And even if she hadn't been…how could he let himself love her again, knowing what that love had cost him?

From the moment they'd met, when Rosa had arrived on the tour bus and introduced herself as the person who'd be documenting their every move for the next month, her presence had filled his whole world, pushing everything else to the edges. The connection had been instantaneous, even if the physical side of their relationship had developed more slowly. Rosa had spoken to them all, of course, taking notes, filming them, her camera always to hand. But somehow, when it had been just the two of them, Jude had found himself giving up far more than she'd asked for—details about his life, his mind, his friendships, his heart. Details she'd never used in the article, because they were just for her.

Whenever the music was done, they'd gravitate towards each other, letting the others head out to party while they headed back to the bus or a hotel room. And soon, all those late-night talks had become midnight kisses, and more, as Jude had lost himself in the wonder of Rosa.

Unbidden, memories of their last night came back to him, filling his brain with the images of them together. The hotel room, the champagne, the post-gig euphoria that always came over him—and Rosa. Rosa's eyes, bright with excitement. Her hair, loose and soft and dark as it hung over her bare shoulders. Her olive skin, so smooth and welcoming under his hands.

The feel of her against him, both of them mindless with the kind of passion Jude knew didn't come around all that often.

Or ever, for him, it seemed, unless it was with Rosa.

It was crazy. He'd been with supermodels, Hollywood actresses—some of the widely acknowledged most beautiful women in the world.

And they'd never made him feel an iota of what he felt in one night with Rosa.

He pushed the memories aside. It was that passion, that uncontrolled connection, that had made him forget the promise he'd made to Gareth after his first close call. Jude had sat beside that hospital bed looking at his best friend—too pale, too lost, so close to being utterly ruined by the drugs and the alcohol and the life it was so easy to live as a band on the road. And he'd

made the most important promise of his life—
he'd promised to keep Gareth safe from then
on. To be the one Gareth could rely on to steer
him away from temptation, to remind him how
much he had to live for.

But then he'd met Rosa and let that promise
slide, too distracted by passion and infatuation
to notice his best friend slipping again.

Until it was too late.

Shaking his head, he looked away as he saw
Sancia putting an arm around Rosa's shoulders
as she led her further into the villa. He had to
stop living in his memories.

He needed to focus on what this meant for
his future.

He'd made a new promise, when Gareth
died—an echo of the one he'd made him a year
before, except *this* one he'd kept, would keep on
keeping. He'd live life for the both of them. He'd
have the success that should have been theirs,
chase the fame Gareth had always wanted. Live
the life Gareth should be there to enjoy.

The Swifts' success wasn't his. It wasn't even
Jimmy's or Lee's or Tanya's. It was all for Gareth.

And that was why he could never walk away
from it. He owed his friend, for the life he got
to live, without him, and for the promise he
should have kept.

But even then, he couldn't stay in New York for the publication of that book.

He'd come to La Isla Marina with a very firm objective in mind—to stay out of the public eye for a few weeks, long enough for all the fuss about *The Naked Truth* to fade away again, and to give him time to think about his next move, musically.

But Rosa being here…that could change everything. He mustn't forget that he'd actually met Rosa when she was photographing the band for some British music magazine. What were the chances she was still doing that sort of work? Just because he hadn't seen her at any of his gigs since didn't mean she wasn't still in the game.

And even if she wasn't, she was a freelance photojournalist. A few shots of Jude Alexander hiding out on a remote Spanish island, when no one else had been able to get a hint of where he was…that would pay big money. Enough for a struggling freelancer to not have to worry about bills for a while, anyway.

Would she sell him out?

Three years ago, Jude could have answered that question without hesitation: never. Rosa wasn't that sort of person. He might have only known her for four weeks, but he'd learned more

about her in one month than he'd known about
his own parents in a lifetime.

And maybe it still meant something. After all,
she hadn't used his secrets in the eventual article
that had been published about that month-long
tour. And there was no mention of Rosa—or
any of the secrets only she knew—in That
Book. There were whole chapters on Gareth,
his death, Jude's guilt over it, and everything
that happened next, but no mention of the part
Rosa had played in everything that happened.

Of course, probably the author just hadn't
known to look for Rosa. If they had…

No, she still wouldn't have talked. She wasn't
that sort of person, he was sure.

But that didn't mean it wasn't worth making
sure she was on the right side of his hide-and-
don't-seek game with the press, before she let
something slip to the wrong person.

The last thing Jude wanted was to have his
hiding place uncovered now, just when his last
remaining secret had walked back into his life.

CHAPTER THREE

'MAMA. MAMA!' Rosa interrupted her mother's non-stop flow of conversation with an impatient shout. It might be rude, but she knew from experience that if she didn't get in there quick before Sancia got lost in one of her conversational tangents, she could be stuck discussing anything but the matter in hand for hours before she got back to the point.

Sancia stopped talking, smiled, then hugged her again.

Rosa hugged her back. Maybe there were some parts of this homecoming that weren't completely awful. Hugs from her mama were definitely one of them. Whatever their family issues, Rosa knew she was lucky to still have her mother in her life. Ten years after she left, Rosa had long forgiven her for walking out on them—understood why she'd needed to, even. Rosa knew that, in her place, she'd have done the same.

If she couldn't fix a situation, couldn't get what she needed from it, she broke free. Just as her mother had done. Just ask Jude.

'I'm sorry, *querida*,' Sancia said, with a warm smile. 'I'm just so excited to have both my girls home with me again.'

Which led Rosa neatly into the first of her very many questions. 'Where *is* Anna, anyway? Jude said something about her going to Barcelona with someone called Leo?' Which seemed utterly unlike her sister, to be honest.

'Ah, you've already met Jude! Isn't he a delight?' Sancia beamed. 'We were so lucky he decided to come and stay here, you know. And he brought your father over with him, for which we are all grateful.'

'He…brought Dad?' Rosa frowned. That made no sense at all. But then, Sancia's ramblings often didn't.

'Well, they arrived together. They travelled over from the mainland in the same boat.' Which was not at all the same thing, Rosa realised.

Sancia didn't always operate on exactly the same plane as everyone else. It wasn't worth explaining the difference—or asking if Sancia had even realised who Jude was. The Swifts wouldn't mean anything to her mother. And she definitely didn't want to mention their past acquaintance.

Which left her with her more immediate concerns.

'So, Mama. Anna. Where is she?'

'Why, Barcelona, like Jude said. With Leo.'

'And Leo is…?' Rosa pressed.

'Anna's…well, not boyfriend, exactly. At least I don't think so. Lover, I suppose.' Sancia sounded far too happy with that answer. Rosa tried to imagine Anna's face if she heard their mother describing any man as her 'lover' and bit back a laugh. 'And he's close to the bride, of course,' Sancia went on, bringing Rosa quickly back to the matter at hand.

'Why don't you tell me more about this wedding, Mama?' she suggested as she manoeuvred her mother further into the villa, towards the small office that sat behind the reception area.

'Of course! You'll need to know all about it,' Sancia agreed, a little too readily for Rosa's liking. 'Anna has left you a list of all the things she needs you to take care of.'

'Has she?' Of course she had. St Anna always did need to be in perfect control of everything. She wouldn't let a little thing like, oh, not actually being there get in the way of that.

Sancia nodded enthusiastically. 'Oh, yes. She's thought of everything. Just look!' She rustled around on the desk until she pulled out a clipboard, with a neatly typed list that, Rosa was almost certain, would prove to contain no typos or grammatical errors.

Although it did seem to contain an awful lot of work to be done.

Rosa took the clipboard from her mother and flipped through the three pages of jobs. 'Seriously? What's *Anna* been doing since she got here?'

'Oh, everything!' Sancia clapped her hands together, pride shining from her eyes. 'She and Leo, they've repainted all the bungalows, tamed the jungle growing out there on the island, fixed all the little things I've been meaning to get around to around here, sorted out the swimming pools for the season…everything!'

'And did she walk on water as well?' Rosa muttered as she looked through *her* list.

'Sorry?' Sancia asked, thankfully unable to make out the words.

'Did they do all that alone?' Rosa asked, instead of repeating her original question.

'Well, Anna's got a whole lot of extra staff coming in this week to help finish it off. But she's organised it all—and been out there with her paintbrush doing more than her fair share!'

Guilt gnawed at Rosa. 'I'm sorry I couldn't get here sooner, Mama.'

'It's fine.' Sancia patted her shoulder. 'You were busy. I understood. And so did your sister.'

That part, Rosa found harder to believe. Even harder than picturing pristine St Anna with a paintbrush in hand.

'Well, she's left me plenty to do to make up for it, anyway.' Rosa stared down at the list again. Then she turned it over so she didn't have to look at it any more. 'So, tell me all about this wedding.'

And why on earth it's sending this whole island into general insanity.

Twenty minutes later, Rosa had her answers. She just didn't like them very much.

'So, when you called and said that there was a wedding booking on the island, what you failed to mention was that it was a five-star, luxury, last-minute wedding for Internet sensation and supermodel Valentina, whose every move is documented online to millions of fans.' A wedding like this could make or break La Isla Marina for the foreseeable future. If they could live up to Valentina's expectations, the resort would be fully booked for years. But if they screwed it up...

That didn't bear thinking about.

Sancia smiled. 'Anna says it's a great opportunity. Apparently Valentina is very popular.'

Understatement. Even in the middle of a South American rainforest, Rosa hadn't been able to avoid Valentina's doings. 'She's about as famous as Jude is.'

Sancia's expression turned curious. 'Jude is famous?'

Oh, honestly. How was she supposed to work like this?

'Just take my word for it, Mama.' She thought about Jude, unrecognised and playing Scrabble with her father. He was hiding. Even if he hadn't fully admitted it yet. 'And maybe don't mention the fact that he's here to anyone, okay?'

'Of course. But Rosa…can you do all these things Anna has asked?' Sancia chewed on her lip, nervously. Because only St Anna could be useful and take care of the family business, right? Only Anna was reliable and dependable—never mind that Sancia had no time at all for those traits usually. Now that she was in trouble, of course it was *Anna* that she needed. Not Rosa.

'I think I can manage a little bit of organisation, for once,' she said, drily. 'Don't worry about it, Mama. I've got you covered.'

She resisted the impulse to look back down at the list and wince. How hard could it be, really? Arranging hotel rooms and putting up decorations was hardly the same as trekking miles through war zones or eluding border patrols, now, was it?

'Oh, good.' Sancia's face relaxed into its usual smiling countenance. 'Then how about I go and fetch you some wine? And some dinner—you must be starving after your journey!'

Rosa knew it wouldn't have mattered what time of day she'd arrived, Sancia would still assume she needed feeding. And a glass of wine. Today though, she wasn't wrong. However, there were a few other things she needed to get straight first.

'In a moment, Mama. You never explained what Dad is doing here.' Rosa remembered what life had been like with both her parents in the same house as a child, and she wasn't sure she wanted to experience it again. For years, Sancia had lived life her way—ignoring her husband's requests for more order in their lives. She'd picked up new creative hobbies that had covered the house in paint or pottery, and brought new friends home to open their lounge up for art classes or book groups. And through it all, Ernest's only comments would be to stay out of his study and clear up after themselves. Rosa wondered, sometimes, if some of the crazier ideas Sancia had come up with—like the midnight picnic in the garden, with fairy lights and music, or the time she'd repainted the whole house yellow, or the last-minute road trip across the country with no preparation or, as it turned out after the first fifty miles, petrol—had just been attempts to get her husband to pay attention to her, for once.

If they had been, they hadn't worked. Even when she'd left, Rosa's father had just increased the time he'd spent at his college, and let Anna take over.

So why was he here, now? And...was Sancia blushing? Really? Rosa was fairly sure her mother had never been embarrassed by anything ever—she just wasn't that sort of person.

Yeah, there was definitely something odd going on here.

'Is it something to do with the wedding?' Rosa pressed. 'Or the island? Is the resort in trouble?' If things were really bad, maybe Sancia had needed to call in the big guns—not just the responsible daughter, but also the ex-husband who'd tried to structure their family lives together to the point of insanity, while Sancia had fought to keep them spontaneous and free-form, until the day she'd left.

Of course, then Anna had taken over organising Rosa's life, so it wasn't as if it had made all that much difference.

But for Mama to call Dad now...

'That's not it at all,' Sancia replied, sounding affronted. Rosa had never been very good at treading carefully around other people's feelings. She suspected it might be a family trait.

'Then why is he here? I mean, now, after all this time?' It had been a full decade since Sancia had left the family home in Oxford. Of course, that was supposed to just be for a holiday—at least, that was what she had told them. And knowing Sancia as Rosa did, she'd probably believed it herself, at the time.

But a holiday had turned into an extended stay—to help her parents out with the resort, all perfectly understandable.

Except for the part where she'd never come home again.

Rosa wasn't even sure her parents had ever officially divorced. It would be just like her mother to leave things completely up in the air as far as officialdom was concerned. And just like her father to refuse to do anything to agree to a situation he hadn't planned for.

They were both as bad as each other, in some ways.

'Your father knew that Anna was here helping me, and he was worried about me,' Sancia said, in such a defensive way that Rosa knew it couldn't be the whole truth.

'And?' she pressed.

'And apparently his cardiologist might have

suggested that it was a good idea, too,' Sancia admitted.

'His cardiologist?' That horrible, guilty feeling was back, clenching around her own heart, as she remembered that last argument with Anna. The one that had started out being about their father's health, and ended up being about *them*, and all the ways they were just too different to ever have that sisterly relationship Rosa had once believed just came from having the same parents.

Of course, since their parents were complete opposites, perhaps it stood to reason that their daughters would be, too.

'Apparently some sun, sea and relaxation are just what he needs—and, of course, La Isla Marina is perfect for that!'

Sun and sea Rosa could agree with. Relaxation seemed an awful long way off right now.

'And you look like you could use some of the same.' Sancia frowned at her youngest daughter, before giving her a little shove towards the door. 'Go on. You go and be nice to our guests, and I'll bring out some food and wine for you all. It'll be a party!'

The headache forming behind Rosa's eyes told her that the last thing she needed was wine, or to spend any more time with the father who had never understood her, or the one man who maybe could have, if she hadn't walked out on him.

But Sancia in hospitality mode was a force to be reckoned with, so it appeared that Rosa didn't have any other choice.

Jude was instantly aware, the moment that Rosa appeared on the patio again. Once, he'd have believed that was a sign of their cosmic connection. Now, he knew it was merely a sign that Rosa was unhappy, and her stamping feet made her flip-flops slap against the tiled floor noisily.

Apparently, questioning her mother hadn't gone well.

'Mama's bringing out food and wine.' Rosa threw herself back into the chair opposite him, the one her father hadn't come back to claim, and tossed a clipboard on top of the Scrabble board between them. 'I couldn't stop her.'

Apparently they were ignoring the tension and difficulties their first conversation in three years had raised, forgetting all about their past connection, and moving on. Well, Rosa always did like to run away from things; maybe he shouldn't be surprised.

And really, it was probably for the best.

'Why would you want to?' Jude asked, following her lead and focussing on the present instead of the past. 'Sancia showing up with food and wine periodically is basically my favourite thing about the island.'

Rosa shrugged. 'Principle, mostly.' He gave her a confused look, and she laughed. 'Let's just call it my contrary nature. Someone tells me I have to go and sit down and make nice with *Melody Magazine*'s Most Gorgeous Man of the Year, while drinking good wine and eating delicious food, and I instantly want to do anything but that."

'That must make life interesting,' Jude said, drily. But a part of him couldn't help wondering if that 'contrary nature' of hers explained a little of their history.

He'd always felt, right from the first, that Rosa was a bit like a wild animal—not one to be tamed, exactly, but one he needed to avoid spooking if he wanted to keep her near.

He just wasn't at all sure what he'd done that had scared her off so much that she'd run away without leaving a forwarding address— and stayed as far away as possible thereafter. His ex, Sylvie, had regularly told him that he was a disaster with women, and she didn't even know about Rosa. He just wished that someone would explain to him what he was supposed to be doing differently.

Except, maybe it wasn't him. Jude leant back in his chair and surveyed Rosa as her gaze flick-

ered from the clipboard on the table, to the archway where Sancia would probably appear from,
to him—ever so briefly—then back to the clipboard again. She chewed on the edge of a nail
as she did so, and her knee didn't stop jiggling
as she sat, sprawled across the chair.

Anyone not watching her carefully might
think, from her posture, that she was as laid-
back as it was possible to be. But Jude, looking
closer, saw more.

Rosa was coiled as tight as a spring, and he
was pretty sure that wasn't his doing. Maybe
her running away that night wasn't entirely his
fault, either.

But right now, whatever was eating her up
was making *him* tense just watching.

'So, what's got you wanting to flee in the
opposite direction right now?' He regretted his
turn of phrase the moment he said it, and he
could tell from the way that Rosa's gaze flew
to his that she had the same, instinctive memory at the words—of her, disappearing from his
bed and running off into the night, without so
much as a goodbye.

She didn't mention it, though. Jude couldn't
quite decide if he was glad about that or not.

'This wedding Mama has agreed to hold on
the island.' Rosa waved a hand towards the clipboard. 'Apparently Anna has run off with her

new *lover*, and left me with all the grunt work.' She dragged out the word 'lover', as if she didn't really believe that was what Leo was.

Jude had seen Anna and Leo together—not intentionally, but they weren't exactly subtle—and he had absolutely no doubt that 'lover' was the right term.

'Who's the wedding for?' he asked, idly. Sancia had mentioned it in passing, when he'd checked in, and he knew Anna had been stressing about it. He'd assumed a family member, or something, but that clipboard had an awful lot of names on it. How big was this thing?

He looked a little closer, and froze as a familiar name caught his eye. *Sylvie Rockwell-Smythe.*

'Valentina.' Rosa sighed. 'Internet sensation, supermodel, millionaire and all-round beautiful person, by all accounts. God only knows why she wanted to hold her wedding *here.*'

Jude knew why. Because he suddenly remembered who told him about La Isla Marina in the first place. Who was responsible for his late-night Internet-searching and his decision to escape to the island.

He'd only met Valentina a handful of times, usually at the sort of event his label loved for him to attend and he tried everything in his power to get out of. But she was a friend of Sylvie's, so when they were in the same place they tended to spend time together. Valentina hadn't been anything like he'd expected her to be—of course, she was beautiful, but so were all the other women at these events. And of course, she was successful, but any suspicion that her fame had been acquired by chance or luck had been dispelled within a few minutes of talking to her.

Valentina was a shrewd businesswoman with a good eye for opportunity. She was curvier and shorter than supermodels were expected to be, but by building her brand online, and tapping into the hashtag, instant-photo-update world, she'd gathered a following that businesses would spend a fortune to access. And they did.

But what had surprised him most, he remembered now, was the night he'd ended up alone at some party with Valentina, late on, when most of the other partygoers had passed out or given up. And she'd spoken, for the first and only time—to him at least—about her childhood in Spain. Growing up as the illegitimate and un-acknowledged daughter of a Spanish aristocrat, watching her mother trying to scrape together a life for them both, any way she could.

'My favourite time was when Mama worked as a cook on this fantastic island resort—La Isla Marina,' Valentina had said. 'I thought it was the most magical place in the world.' The name

had stuck in his head, and when he'd been looking to escape for a while, he'd plugged it into
a search engine and been on a plane less than
twenty-four hours later.

Why hadn't he remembered that sooner? And
if he had, would it even have made any difference?

He hadn't thought for a moment that Valentina would plan a trip here, too. Yes, she had
fond memories of the place, but that wasn't the
same as relocating her entire wedding there—
especially since, last time he'd had an update on
the wedding planning from Sylvie, when they
were still together, Valentina and Todd were
getting married in some top-notch, luxury villa
somewhere. Between them, Todd and Valentina
could afford any wedding venue in the world.
So why were they coming *here*?

Maybe this was fate. Destiny's way of making him deal with all the things about his life,
his future, his whole existence that he'd been
putting off for too long. The breakup with Sylvie and the book's release had lit the fire under
him, and now look where he was—stuck in the
middle of nowhere with the one woman he'd
thought he could love, and the one he knew he
couldn't arriving imminently. That definitely
felt as if the universe was sending him a mes-
sage about dealing with his issues.

Except, just in case some more earthly powers were behind this unlikely coincidence, Jude decided it was worth asking at least one practical follow-up question. Especially since he knew La Isla Marina wasn't Valentina's first wedding venue choice—however nostalgic she was for the place.

'I thought Valentina was getting married out in some incredible luxury villa somewhere?' Somewhere very much else.

'Apparently it burnt down.' Rosa sighed. 'Which is very sad, obviously, but she seems to have decided to move the whole shebang here, decorations and all, despite never even doing a site visit.'

Because she had it all in her memory, of course. But Jude wasn't going to spill Valentina's secrets for her.

'Well, I'm sure she'll love it here,' Jude said, trying not to look around him for evidence to the contrary. He knew what sort of luxury Valentina and her friends were used to and, despite all the hard work Anna and Leo seemed to be putting in to get the bungalows up to scratch, Jude had to admit that La Isla Marina wasn't quite the magical paradise that Valentina seemed to remember. Yet, anyway.

'Not right now, she wouldn't,' Rosa said bluntly. She'd worked around celebrities, of course. She knew the expectations, too. 'Mama says that Anna's arranged for an army of seasonal staff—including a plumber, joiner and builder—to arrive tomorrow and finish off the work of making the accommodation decent.'

'Well, that's good, isn't it?' The way Rosa said it, he suspected not.

'I suppose. Except it means that I'm left with all the wedding stuff. Allocating accommodation for the guests, decorating the pagoda, working out seating plans, dealing with what is sure to be their many, many issues when they arrive.'

'And you'd rather be painting?' Jude guessed.

'I'd rather be thousands of miles away with my camera, chasing a good story.' She gave him a half-smile, as if to indicate that she was joking—which Jude was pretty sure she wasn't. 'It's just that this sort of thing—admin and paperwork and people—it's not really playing to my strengths. I'm better with a paintbrush in hand.'

'So why has Anna given these jobs to you?'

'Punishment, I reckon. For showing up two weeks after she did.' Rosa sighed, and pulled the clipboard towards her. 'I mean, look at some of these names. Tyrana Lichfield-Burrows. Ursula Pennington. Isadora-Marie Woodford-Williams, for heaven's sake. Do they sound like my sort of people?'

'Actually, Isadora-Marie is nice. And funny. But I can tell you now you're going to hate Ursula.' It was a flippant remark, but Jude realised his mistake almost instantly.

Rosa's gaze sharpened, fastened on his face as she leant across the table towards him. 'You know these people,' she said, in the sort of voice he'd never been able to lie to.

Wincing, Jude nodded, reluctantly. 'Yes.'

CHAPTER FOUR

ROSA SMILED. This guest list featured some of New York's most celebrated and fabulous citizens—*of course* Jude, rock-star celebrity, would know them. And probably know them well enough to be able to tell her who shouldn't be sat next to whom, and which of them were likely to cause the most trouble. She might not like doing the admin and organising side of things—she'd always been more of the 'make it up as you go along' type, like her mother—but if she *had* to do it, then some insider knowledge would most definitely prove helpful.

'You can help me, then,' she said, and saw Jude wince again. What was the problem? These were his friends—he should be looking forward to seeing them. Except…she flipped through the guest list. 'Hang on, why aren't you invited to this shindig?'

Jude sighed. 'Probably because one of the bridesmaids broke up with me six weeks ago.'

'Sylvie. Right.' That might explain all the wincing. 'So, was it her or the book that you ran all the way to Spain to escape from?'

'Bit of both,' Jude murmured, but didn't elaborate.

'I guess you won't be staying for the wedding, then?' At least his answer had proved her right about one thing—Jude *was* hiding. But how bad an ex-girlfriend were they talking about that he had to run away to a decrepit Spanish island to escape her?

Mind you, she'd run to the other end of the earth to escape him, and he'd been pretty much perfect.

Of course, that was why she'd run. Perfection was terrifying—especially in the face of all her faults.

'Depends, I guess,' Jude said. Then he shook his head. 'I honestly don't know. I came here to get away from everything, but now…maybe this is meant to be. Maybe it's time to face some demons from my past.'

His gaze caught hers as he said it, and suddenly Rosa felt the knowledge that they weren't just talking about his ex, or some book any more weighing heavy on her heart.

She'd tried not to think too much about Jude after she left—that way, she was pretty sure, madness lay. Or at best, running back to him, just when she'd escaped his thrall. Rosa wasn't the sort to dwell. She moved on, got over it and kept going. That was all she knew.

He talked about being here to face his demons as if it were a good thing. If Rosa had the choice, she'd be running as fast as she could in the opposite direction from everything and everyone on La Isla Marina.

'So…you're planning on staying?' Rosa asked, surprised. 'And I kind of have to stay.' At least, if she wanted her family to speak to her ever again. Although she'd gone three years without that from Anna and her father already… No. Rosa didn't have so much family that she could be *quite* that cavalier about losing them.

'So we're both here. On the island. For the duration.' Jude's gaze was heavy and meaning-ful, and Rosa had an awful feeling she knew exactly where he wanted this conversation to go: back to the night she left, and searching for explanations why.

Yeah, she really wasn't ready to have that talk yet. Let him deal with his other demons—what-ever they were—first, and come back to her last. Like when someone was taking for ever to make up their mind choosing from the menu in a restaurant, and asked the waiter to ask them again at the end.

But Jude wasn't a waiter. And if she couldn't

avoid Jude any longer, she might as well take advantage of the fact he was there. Apart from anything else, giving him something else to focus on—like the impending arrival of his ex—might distract him from their own past. And honestly? She could use the help.

Pasting on a bright smile, she ignored the vibes and merrily changed the subject. 'Great! Well, in that case, you can definitely help me out with all these tasks Anna's left for me. I'm sure your insider knowledge will be invaluable.'

Jude didn't seem particularly excited at the prospect. In fact, he didn't look as if he wanted to change the subject at all.

'Rosa. Don't you think we need to talk—?'

'Not really,' she said, honestly. 'I think we were friends, three years ago, before anything else. Maybe we can be that again. I have too much to focus on here for this wedding to even think about anything else right now.'

He didn't agree with her; she could see it in his face. Jude was the talking sort, and she, well, wasn't. Not unless she had to be.

But then, just as Jude opened his mouth to argue, Sancia appeared in the doorway, holding a tray of tapas and flanked by Rosa's father, carrying wine.

She had, quite seriously, never been so pleased to see her parents in her whole life.

'Mama! Dad!' She jumped up from her chair and bounced across the courtyard to help them with the plates. Her father in particular looked surprised at the welcome. Understandably, she supposed. They'd never been affectionate, the two of them. Professor Gray kept even people he loved and liked, like Sancia or Anna, at arm's length, and he'd never known what to make of his younger, wilder daughter. It was as if blood was the only thing they'd ever had in common.

Until now. Now, they all had the future of La Isla Marina in common. And she and her father had the added connection of Jude's friendship.

Now, they were all going to have to try and get along for a while.

And they could start by getting her out of a very awkward conversation with Jude. 'Why don't you come and join us? Jude has lots of questions about the island.'

Once Sancia got talking about La Isla Marina, it would be impossible for anyone to get a word in edgeways. Especially if that word was the one question Rosa really didn't want to answer. *Why?*

Because, seeing Jude again, all of her reasons had already started to fade away. And she couldn't afford to let that happen. Not when she knew she was leaving again, as soon as this wedding was over.

* * *

Jude awoke the next morning to the sound of the sea lapping against the rocks outside his bungalow window, the sun already shining through the thin gauze curtains. He lay for a moment just enjoying the peace, the solitude and the beauty of La Isla Marina.

And then his brain caught up with his body.

Rosa was here. Sylvie was coming here. And he'd promised to spend his day helping Rosa prepare for the socialite wedding of the year.

Just perfect.

His head suddenly aching, Jude forced himself out of bed and into the shower. So much for his idyllic secret getaway. From the look of Rosa's clipboard, half of Manhattan was now following him there. And it wasn't even the half he really *liked*.

Letting the water sluice over his skin, Jude thought back over the strange events of the day before. Had he been imagining it, or had Rosa been trying to avoid talking about their history together? She certainly hadn't let on to her parents how close they'd been, once. Instead, she'd talked about him as just one more subject she'd photographed and written about.

Maybe that was all he was, to her.

Could he have imagined that connection between them? That instantaneous, shocking attraction?

Had she just been patiently listening three years ago, as he'd poured out his heart to her, in the hope that she'd find a good story?

No.

He shook water droplets from his hair as he stepped out of the shower, letting the warm Spanish air dry his skin.

He'd seen the same confusion and amazement in Rosa's eyes, that first night they'd been together. That overwhelmed, overtaken look that had echoed exactly how he'd felt.

She'd been as rocked by their connection as he had. She'd just reacted differently.

And maybe now the universe was giving him the chance to find out why—whether she wanted to tell him or not.

Rosa might have distracted him last night with Sancia's tales of the island, and the truly excellent wine and tapas she provided. But today was another day—and they'd already arranged to meet at the villa to go over the guest list and arrangements.

Jude smiled to himself as he pulled on his dark linen trousers and a crisp white linen shirt. If Rosa wanted his help, she'd better be prepared to pay in her secrets.

Especially since she already knew all of his.

* * *

The villa was deserted when he reached Reception, so Jude loitered in the cool shade of the tiled reception hall. The white painted arches overhead and the cool vistas reminded him more of a Middle Eastern palace than a Spanish villa, but he liked the feel of the place. It felt as if time had stopped, or at least slowed to a lazy, honey-slow meander. After the bustle of New York City, Jude was enjoying the change of pace.

Sancia had told him the romantic tale of how the island came to her in her family the night before: how Sancia's grandparents had built the villa as their retreat from the world when they married, and how Sancia's parents had built the resort around it when they inherited it. At one time, it was supposed to have been a jewel in the Med, *the* place for the movers and shakers of the time to be seen.

He supposed it would be again, soon. If they got all the necessary work done on time.

Jude was about to reach across the reception desk to pick up the phone and see if there was a direct line to the office, or someone—anyone—who might know where Rosa was, when she suddenly appeared before him.

He blinked. 'Where did you come from?'

'Mama didn't show you the secret door, then,

when she gave you the tour?' Rosa grinned. 'Good. A girl has to have some secrets.'

'Secret door?' Jude honestly couldn't tell if she was teasing him or not. 'Are you kidding?'

Rosa shook her head. 'Nope! There's a secret door somewhere in this reception hall that leads to the family quarters. How else are we poor staff supposed to get some peace and quiet from all you demanding guests?'

'I'm going to spend my entire stay trying to figure out whether you're making this up or not,' Jude admitted, which made Rosa's grin grow even wider.

'I'm okay with that,' she answered.

'So, where do we start today?' Jude nodded at the clipboard in Rosa's hands. 'Want to go through and see how many names I recognise? Or how about you run me through the schedule for the week, see if I can highlight any potential danger zones.' If he was here to be useful, he might as well make an effort. And by pure osmosis—and listening to Sylvie gossip—he thought he could probably offer some pretty good insights. Who was likely to abuse the free bar and might need to be kept away from the sea afterwards. Who would find something to complain about regardless, so it was worth giving them a tiny flaw in their bungalow that was easily fixed, just so they'd feel happy. Hell, he even knew one of the bridesmaids was allergic to fresh-cut flowers!

How much of his brain had been taken over by this world—Sylvie's world? The world of celebrity that his label wanted him to be seen in.

What had happened to the music being the most important thing?

'All of those sound like great ideas,' Rosa said. 'But actually... I thought we might take a walk around the island, first. I kind of want to see what Anna's been doing here for the last two weeks, and get an idea of what shape we're in, before I get down to the nitty-gritty stuff.'

'Makes sense,' Jude said. 'Of course, it also sounds like a total procrastination attempt to avoid doing the *actual* work Anna left you...'

Rosa hit him in the arm with her clipboard, not hard enough to hurt, but enough to make him shut up and grin at her.

This was interesting. Last time they'd met, they'd been on his home turf—as much as a band tour bus could be called anyone's home. They'd been in his world, before The Swifts had really hit the mainstream and started playing stadiums instead of pubs and tiny music venues. He'd known his place there, in a way he didn't quite, these days.

But this time, they were on Rosa's patch—her family home, even, for all that it was also an island resort. This was the place she ran to when they called—rather than running away.

And that meant he got to see a whole other side of Rosa, this time. Maybe he'd even see enough to understand why she left.

Rosa led them out of the villa, down the long, straight path that led back to the jetty and escape from the island. But before they reached the sea, she took a sharp right down a narrower path, through recently cut-back lush greenery. It was the opposite direction from Jude's own bungalow, but, still, things looked familiar.

The bungalows they passed were just like the one he was staying in—low and white, half hidden between the plants and brightly coloured flowers. The smell of fresh paint lingered as they got closer to one; Jude knew that even a few days ago many of them had been grey and dingy. One or two he'd seen on his rambles across the island had displayed broken roof tiles and wooden shutters that hung from their hinges.

Not now, though.

Now, every bungalow gleamed in the sunlight, the freshly painted shutters giving a splash of colour against the white walls. The jungle Jude had fought his way through on arrival had been tamed, so the island looked lush, fresh and green, rather than overtaken by plants. Even the patios outside the bungalows had been swept, scrubbed, and the iron patio furniture cleaned and looking ready for use.

It was quite the transformation. If Jude had been paying more attention to the island, rather than his own thoughts—and Scrabble games— he would have noticed sooner. As it was, suddenly he could see what had drawn Valentina to the island.

Rosa was surveying it with a more critical eye. 'How bad was it? Before the work started, I mean.'

Jude shrugged. 'It was already pretty far under way when I arrived.'

'But some parts weren't done yet, right? What did they look like?'

'They were…' He winced as he tried to find the words to describe how run-down and derelict parts of the island had looked, just a week or so ago.

'That bad, huh?'

'Worse,' he admitted. 'Anna and Leo—and their crew—have done an incredible job around here.'

Rosa let out a long sigh. 'Then she's going to be even more unbearable when she gets back.'

'What do you mean?' Jude dropped to sit on the cast-iron chair on the patio of the nearest bungalow. Motioning across the table, he indicated for Rosa to take the other seat.

'We should have brought coffee with us,' she grumbled as she sat.

Having tasted Sancia's coffee, Jude definitely agreed. But getting Rosa to talk about herself, that was good, too.

Part of him wondered why he still cared—why it still mattered to him at all. It had been three years since she'd left him, and it wasn't as if they'd had a lengthy relationship before that. It had been a short, hot fling—and if he had any sense at all, he'd just keep the memory of that and move on.

Why had he expected anything else, anything more? Because it had felt so real, while it was happening. And like a dream once it was over.

There'd been women since, of course—short-term and long-term. And his life had changed beyond all measure—the tour bus replaced with a private jet, and the grim pubs they'd played with hundred-thousand-seater stadiums. His music was recognised, loved, had gone double platinum—twice. The band had grown closer still, as they'd gone through all the changes together. Especially after they'd lost Gareth. They all knew they had to take care of each other, in a way they hadn't been able to take care of Gareth. In the way he *should* have taken care of Gareth.

But somehow, Jude had become the star—more recognisable than his bandmates, the one the papers and magazines wanted to interview, to photograph. The one who drew the rumours and the stories and the lies.

Still. He had so many people in his life now—from bandmates to friends to acquaintances to his agent to the people at the label to the *über*-fans—that Rosa should have faded from his consciousness completely. He shouldn't even have *recognised* her when she walked in last night.

But he'd known her voice in an instant.

Maybe it was just that he knew what had gone wrong with every other relationship in his life—but Rosa's motives for leaving remained a mystery. But deep down, Jude knew it was more than that.

He'd opened his heart and his soul to this woman, let her see everything that he was. She was the only person he'd ever done anything close to that for—besides Gareth. But Gareth had been his best friend since they were three. He'd known Rosa less than a month. And still, she was the only person in the world that had seen every inch of the real him. The only one to know him at all, once Gareth died.

And she'd run away. What did that say about the real him?

No wonder he hadn't let anyone else so close since.

He wanted to know her as well as she'd known him, then. Wanted to understand her—find what was wrong with him, or with her, that she'd left and never looked back.

Starting with her obviously acrimonious relationship with her sister.

'So. What's the deal with you and your sister?'

Rosa stared mutinously at him. 'We're sisters. What do you expect?'

Jude thought about his cousins—three sisters who were so close they could practically read each other's mind. 'I guess all sibling relationships are different.'

'You're an only child,' she pointed out, and Jude felt a small jolt as he realised she'd remembered that small fact about him. 'What would you know?'

She was right, he supposed. He'd had Gareth, but that wasn't the same. They'd grown up together, sure, but they hadn't had the same parents, lived the same life in the same place, not until they were eighteen.

'So tell me,' he suggested.

Rosa sighed. 'Anna and I...there's only two

years between us, but sometimes it feels more like decades.'

'You're not very alike?'

'Physically? Sure—we both look like Mama, in case you hadn't noticed.'

He tried to remember what Anna looked like; he'd only met her briefly a couple of times since he arrived. Obviously she couldn't look too like Rosa or he might have noticed sooner. 'I suppose…' he said, slowly. 'I mean, yes, you look like Sancia. And so does Anna. And yet, I never looked at Anna and thought she looked like you.' And he would have done. He'd spent three years looking for Rosa in strangers.

'Dad used to say that when you looked at the two of us in photos we could be twins,' Rosa said, sounding a little wistful. 'It was only when you saw us in motion that it became clear we were completely different people.'

Jude tilted his head to look at Rosa, taking in her slouched posture, one ankle resting on her knee. Her long, dark hair hung over one shoulder in some sort of complicated braid, and she was watching him from under long, dark lashes.

She was trying to look relaxed, he realised. And maybe to other people she'd look that way. But Jude could almost feel the tension coming off her in waves—the same as last night.

With another sigh, she sat upright again, leaning her elbows forward onto the patio table. 'The thing is, Anna was always Dad's favourite. She's just like him, really—all academic and serious and organised and stuff. And me, I'm more like Mama. A free spirit.'

'That's why you don't get on?' Jude asked. 'Too different?'

'Partly.' She bit her lip, bright white teeth sharp against the lushness of her mouth. Jude felt a jolt of lust rush through him as he remembered the last time he'd seen her do that. She'd been sitting astride him at the time...

He swallowed. Hard. 'What else?' Focussing on the facts, that was what mattered now.

He was going to learn why Rosa left him. He was going to understand, finally, the terrible string of events that led to Gareth's death. And then he was going to turn around and leave her, and any influence she had on his life, behind. Move on himself, at last. That was the plan and he was sticking to it. Memories be damned.

'My mother left us. I must have told you that?' She looked at him, waited for him to nod a confirmation before she carried on. 'Before then life was...balanced, I guess. Dad would spend all his time at the university, or in his study, only appearing to complain about the state of the house, or to try and install some sort of order into our lives. And Mama...she just concentrated on us all being happy. She didn't care if we arrived at the beach without the picnic, or our swimming costumes. We'd have ice cream for lunch and swim in our knickers.'

'They were the ultimate in opposites attracting, then?' Jude guessed.

'Pretty much.' Rosa gave him a lopsided smile. 'But it worked, you know? At least, until it didn't.'

'What happened?'

Rosa sighed. 'Can we walk while I tell this story? I talk better when I'm moving.'

He remembered that, Jude realised. All those nights cramped on the tour bus, and it was always him whispering secrets and telling his soul. Rosa only started to talk when they escaped—when they ran down Southend pier at night together, or explored the streets of London, just the two of them. That was when he got to hear the inner workings of Rosa's heart.

'Where do you want to go?' he asked, getting to his feet.

Rosa had already jumped up, and was halfway down the track. 'To the sea, of course,' she said, the words tossed back over her shoulder.

Jude didn't mention that he'd had enough of the sea on his crossing from the mainland, or that his bungalow was right next to the shore. Why wasn't he surprised that Rosa—shiftless, always moving Rosa—was drawn to the ocean, with all its ebbs and flows and tides?

At least the sea was predictable, to a point. Except for tsunamis and stuff.

Even they seemed more predictable than Rosa.

Jude kept quiet and waited for her to start talking again as they walked. He caught up easily, and walked beside her on the narrow path that wound across the island, down to the shore.

Eventually, she spoke.

'When Mama left…she didn't exactly walk out. That's not Mama's style, really—a monumental decision and a fight and a definite end.'

'So what did she do?' Jude couldn't quite quash the hope that somewhere in the story of why Sancia left Ernest Gray would be the explanation for her daughter's hit-and-run attitude.

'She came here, to La Isla Marina, for a holiday.' Rosa's smile was too tight, too fixed. 'It was only supposed to be for a week or two. She left Anna and me with Dad.'

'How old were you?'

'Sixteen. Anna was eighteen. About to sit her A-levels.'

'And you must have had your GCSEs,' Jude pointed out.

'Yeah. But they didn't matter in the same way. Anna was always the academic one.' Rosa shook her head. 'Anyway. Two weeks turned into a month. Mama said that our grandparents needed her help—that running the resort was too much for them now they were getting older. And it wasn't a lie—I mean, you saw this place when you arrived. But…somehow, she just never came home again.'

Jude's heart ached for this girl who'd lost the only family member who made her feel as if she belonged. 'I can't imagine how that must have hurt.'

Rosa shrugged. 'It wasn't so much Mama leaving, I don't think. I mean, I visited her out here every holiday and, to be honest, the weeks I spent here on the island were the happiest I remember. And *she* was so much happier here. It wasn't until she left that I saw the truth—how unhappy, how stifled she'd been in Oxford, surrounded by people who needed academic proofs and publications to back up their every feeling.'

'People like Anna and your dad.'

'Exactly! Mama was never like that. She was all impulse and fun and living life in colour. She needed to be free.'

'Like you.' Because that was always how he'd remembered Rosa. Full colour. Even when he felt stuck in black-and-white noir.

'Maybe.' She gave him a sidelong look. 'Anyway, with Mama gone, it was just Dad and

Anna. And Dad retreated back into his office again, so Anna took over everything else. Running the household, organising Dad, and ordering me around.'

Jude winced. 'I'm guessing that didn't go down so well with you.'

'You guess right.' Rosa sighed. 'The worst thing is, now, with ten years of hindsight, I can't even blame her completely. We were both trying to cope with a monumental change in our lives, and I guess we each did it differently. But then… I just felt so hemmed in and frustrated. Before then, we'd always got on well. Yes, we were different, but we were sisters and we were close. It was us against the parents, you know? But when Mama left…'

'It was you against Anna.'

'And it has been ever since.' Rosa pushed a last, stray branch out of their path, then moved ahead of him, her long braid swaying in time to her hips. It was almost hypnotising. As if she could take over his mind just in the way she moved. Which, on past evidence, wasn't entirely untrue. 'We haven't spoken in three years, now.'

Then she stopped in front of him, so suddenly he almost crashed into her. Jude's hands came up, ready to grab her hips for balance, but at the last moment he realised the insanity of that plan and held onto the nearest tree, instead.

Rosa breathed in deeply, her shoulders moving with the motion. 'I miss the sea, when I'm away. Other oceans don't smell quite the same.'

'It must be strange to be home, with your whole family here.' Jude let Rosa step out onto the small beach in the cove they'd arrived at. It was secluded, idyllic and, under other circumstances, wildly romantic.

'Very,' Rosa admitted. 'There are so many memories tied up in this place…' She trailed off, then gave a low laugh.

'What?'

'Talking of memories, I just realised where we are,' she said. 'This is the beach where I lost my virginity.'

CHAPTER FIVE

ROSA REGRETTED IT the moment she said it. *When* would she learn to think before she spoke? When she was little, her father had always told her she needed to learn that lesson more than any other, before she grew up. Now she was twenty-six, she was starting to think that it might be a permanent condition.

What else could explain her impulse to mention sex in front of the one man she was busy pretending she had never slept with?

She glanced quickly at Jude's face, looking away almost instantly to stare out over the sea. This was one of her favourite spots on the island—always had been. That was why she'd chosen it for what she'd imagined would be a memorable night—her first time.

It was memorable, she supposed, if not entirely for the right reasons. It had basically been a disaster.

Much like the conversation she felt coming.

Jude came to stand beside her, close enough

that his arm brushed against hers. His skin was too pale, Rosa thought, looking at it next to her own. As if he'd been locked away somewhere, forced to make music and never see sunlight.

No wonder he'd felt he needed to run away to a sunny island in the middle of nowhere.

'Talking about sex,' Jude said, his voice soft, his gaze fixed on the horizon. 'Are we ever going to?'

'Have sex?' Rosa's voice came out squeaky, even as she realised that *of course* that wasn't what he meant.

'Talk about it. What happened between us.' He turned his head to look at her, and his bright blue gaze seemed to see right through her clothes, her skin, deep into the heart of her.

That was the problem with Jude. He always saw too deep.

'Why you left,' he added, and Rosa broke away from his gaze.

'Do we have to?' she asked, kicking at the sand with the front of her flip-flop.

Jude's cool fingers came under her chin, lifting her face so she had to look at him again. 'Rosa… I can't help but think that I'm here on this island for a reason. To find closure, on all kinds of things—starting with what happened between us, and everything that happened afterwards. And if you want us to work together on this wedding, I think we're going to have to, you know...'

'Have the talk.' Rosa sighed. Why couldn't she have fallen for one of the roadies, or even one of his bandmates like Jimmy, three years ago? Most men she met would run a thousand miles rather than talk about their feelings—which suited Rosa just fine, thanks.

But no, she had to go and fall for the sensitive artist. The one person who wanted to *understand* her.

Even if she didn't want to be understood. Even if she didn't understand herself, sometimes.

'I'll do you a deal,' Jude said, his voice more normal suddenly—as if they weren't talking about sex and love any more. 'You tell me what happened that night—why you left, and why you never came back. You help me understand that, and we never have to talk about it again, okay? We can just be acquaintances—friends, even—spending time together on a holiday island. Okay?'

'Okay,' Rosa said, slowly. It sounded good, she had to admit.

The only problem was, for all her brave words, she couldn't imagine ever being friends with Jude Alexander. Not after what they'd shared.

But she was willing to try if he was.

Taking a few steps forward towards the sea, she kicked off her flip-flops and sat on the edge of the sand, letting the waves lap over her toes.

Leaning back on her hands, Rosa shut her eyes. The warm sun on her skin felt like home. Like love.

'So,' she asked, her eyes still closed. 'What do you want to know?'

She felt rather than saw Jude settle beside her, and wondered if he'd taken off his shoes, too. Maybe even rolled up those dark linen trousers. He might have a slender, rock-star frame, but his shoulders were broader than you'd think, and there were muscles on that frame, too, she remembered. Could almost see through his thin white shirt if she didn't concentrate on not looking…

She opened her eyes. Jude had his bare feet in the water, just like her. Rosa smiled. Good. He needed to relax more.

'Was it something I did?' he asked, staring out at the sea. 'Or did you just not feel the same way I did?'

Rosa swallowed, tasting regret in her mouth. 'How did you feel?'

'Like magic had walked into my life, the moment I met you,' Jude said, simply. 'Like I'd been waiting for you for centuries.'

Guilt pierced through Rosa's heart. She knew exactly what he meant, and *of course* she'd felt it, too. But how could she tell him that was the whole problem? That sort of perfection wasn't meant for the mess that was her. She'd screw it up sooner or later, and sooner was better, in her experience.

'And that's why you're the songwriter of the two of us,' she joked, her heart breaking as she said it. 'You can take a tour-bus fling and make it into poetry.'

'Is that all we were?' Jude shifted on the sand so he could look at her, almost lying down on his side as he spoke. 'A tour-bus fling?'

God, but it was so tempting to curl up there with him, safe in his arms. But Rosa knew she might not have the strength to leave them twice.

'We knew each other for four weeks, Jude,' she reminded him, gently.

'I knew all I needed to in the first day.'

She remembered. Remembered the way their eyes had met and she'd just *known*. Known that this man was going to be important.

Rosa didn't believe in love at first sight, but if she had…

She shook her head. What difference did it make if it was love or not? That didn't change everything else that it was.

A burden. A chain. A prison.

She'd seen what happened when a woman fell in love—so deeply in love that she gave up all her own dreams and moved to Oxford to live his life, instead of hers. She'd seen her mother live it, so she didn't have to. Twenty years of frustration and bitterness, followed by her finally leaving for her island refuge.

Rosa had known, even then, that she wasn't willing to live that life. Wasn't willing to compromise her own dreams one bit to live someone else's.

She needed to end this now. She needed to tell Jude enough to get him to stop asking—to give him his closure. Then they could both move on, and she'd be as free of him as he was of her.

That was what she wanted. It was all she ever wanted: freedom.

'I told you why at the time,' she said. 'I had to come home for my *abuelo*—for my grandfather's—funeral.'

'Except you didn't tell me where home was,' Jude reminded her. 'Or that you weren't coming back.'

And there was the sticking point. She hadn't really known that, at the time. It was only once she was out of Jude's sphere, without his smile or his hands or his eyes influencing her decisions, that she realised the risk. When she knew that she had to stay away.

That, and a terrifying two weeks when her body told her she might have made a monumental, life-changing mistake, that first, impulsive night she'd spent with him.

As she'd waited, too scared to even buy a pregnancy test and know for sure, too distraught dealing with all the funeral stuff to even really think about it, one thing had been abundantly clear to her.

If she went back to Jude when she left La Isla Marina, that would be it. If four weeks in each other's company, in his bed, could have this kind of impact on her life, her heart, then going back would be a life sentence.

She'd fall irrevocably in love with him, and never be able to break away. She'd live her mother's life—following him around the world as he toured, always being his plus one, and never finding her own life, her own self. Her own happiness.

Or worse, she'd be Anna—managing Jude's personal life as Anna managed Dad's, giving up her own opportunities and possibilities to him.

She couldn't do that. Couldn't sacrifice all her dreams for his dream of stardom.

And she'd had no doubt that Jude would be a star—anyone who'd heard The Swifts play had known that it was only a matter of time before they made it big. And Jude and Gareth, they'd made a pact, when they were barely teenagers, that one day they'd be famous together. They'd escape all the people who told them they'd never make anything of themselves, the families and schools who told them it was impossible. They were going to conquer the world together—and they'd already been so close, when Rosa met them. She knew it wouldn't be long until the name Jude Alexander was on everyone's lips.

Would he even want her around, then? When beautiful women were throwing themselves at him, and every door was open to him?

By the time her cycle had returned—delayed by stress, rather than her carelessness in bed with Jude, it seemed—the funeral was long over and Rosa had made a decision.

She needed to find her own life, her own happiness. She wouldn't make her mother's mistakes all over again, falling for a man whose career would always come first, who would forget she existed for weeks at a time.

And so she'd run as far away as she could—and ended up back here with him three years later, anyway.

Looking at him, Rosa knew the risk was still there. If she let herself get too close to Jude, let herself hope, she could fall anyway, despite all the distance she'd put between them. And if she gave him a hint that she still felt that way...

So she had to lie. Or at least, not tell the whole truth.

'Honestly?' she said, knowing she was being anything but honest. 'I hadn't decided when I left what I was going to do next. But then an opportunity came up for a new commission out in the Middle East, and it sounded interesting so…' She shrugged. 'You know me. I like to keep moving, finding new experiences, seeking out the next big thing.'

Jude grabbed her hand suddenly, making her turn to face him, staring into her eyes as if he could see the truth behind them. Rosa held her nerve, ignoring her heart beating too fast in her chest, and let him look. Nothing she had said was *technically* untrue, after all.

'So, is that what I was?' Jude asked, after a moment. 'Just another new experience?'

No. He'd been *the* experience. The one she judged every other moment of her life against. And all too often found them lacking.

No other man had ever lived up to four weeks with Jude. And yes, she'd had regrets, had imagined what could have been.

And he couldn't know that. Because regrets didn't change anything. The only way she knew how to move was forward.

Rosa gave an apologetic shrug, and Jude dropped her hand.

'So, does every experience have to be new?' He'd gone back to staring at the sea again now, and Rosa's heart had started to settle back down to a normal rhythm. Maybe that was why she didn't think carefully enough about her response. As usual.

'Some are worth experiencing twice,' she admitted, her words coming out soft and husky.

Jude's gaze snapped back to hers, and she saw the lust there. The want. The *need*.

And the worst thing was she was almost sure her eyes were reflecting the same feelings right back at him.

Rosa leapt to her feet. 'Right! We should get back to work.'

'Work.' Jude shook his head. 'Sure.'

She'd given him the answers he wanted, and now he owed her his help with this damn wedding.

And if Rosa wished she could have told him the truth?

She'd get over it. She'd move on.

She always did.

Jude stared at the room full of boxes, all with comprehensive shipping labels stuck on them.

Somehow, the resolution he'd made to be all business with Rosa was coming back to bite him. He'd *almost* rather live through that soul-crushing conversation with Rosa on the beach all over again than sort through fifty boxes of wedding decorations and accessories.

But only almost. He wasn't sure he could take hearing Rosa tell him how he was just one more experience again.

It wasn't as if he hadn't known she was a free spirit back then—it was one of the things he liked most about her, the way she surged forward after her own life, not caring about schedules or plans or what other people thought.

She was the way he'd always thought *he* was, until he realised how much of his life was organised by other people.

Music—that was supposed to be the ultimate freedom, wasn't it? Creating something from nothing, something from inside the soul, something that touched millions of others. It was supposed to be his escape—from a town with no work, a father who told him he was a waste of space and a school that told him he had no future. He and Gareth had dreamed of the day they'd prove them all wrong—and they'd never doubted they could do it, together.

Music was *their* thing. The one thing in the world that no one could take away from them. But then the world, and addiction, had taken Gareth away from him. Maybe that was why he felt sometimes as if it wasn't his at all, any more.

That was why he'd come to La Isla Marina—to find his freedom again. The fact that he'd found the one person chaining him to his memories of the past was beside the point.

Jude knew it all came down to what happened with Gareth. It was all tangled together in his head—the promise he'd made, and broken. If Rosa hadn't been there, he'd have seen the signs sooner. He'd have been at whichever party it was when Gareth decided just one more hit wouldn't hurt. He'd have noticed one becoming two becoming every night again.

Gareth had overdosed less than a month after Rosa left, and Jude knew that if he hadn't been so focussed on his own pain during that month he would have noticed Gareth's. The events were all tied up together, running together like two melodies in his head, twisting together to make a new song. However much he told himself that Gareth's addiction wasn't his fault, wasn't Rosa's fault for leaving, he knew he was the only person in the world who could have stopped it.

He knew he'd always blame himself for his friend's death, more than the drugs that had caused it. Because when Gareth had needed him, Jude had been too caught up in Rosa to even notice. He'd broken the most important promise he'd ever made—the promise he'd made in that hospital room, a year before Gareth died, that he'd be there for him. That he'd keep his friend safe.

He shook his head, and tried to focus on the task in hand. Gareth was gone. All Jude could do now was live their dream for both of them. Enjoy the success Gareth had craved, and the high life he'd looked forward to so much. Show the world that had dismissed them that they could do anything—even if the price they had to pay seemed far, far too high.

And as for Rosa... He had the closure he'd asked for, at last. He knew why she left—however much he didn't like it.

Now he had to keep up his end of the bargain. Which apparently involved wedding decorations and accessories.

'Did you count them yet?' Rosa asked, clipboard in hand. 'Anna's notes say there should be fifty.'

'What could Valentina possibly need for her wedding that requires fifty boxes?' Jude asked as he started counting again. Just the sight of Rosa in her tight jeans, rolled up to show off slim ankles, and her close-fitting white T-shirt was enough to make him lose count.

'Everything, according to these lists.' Rosa stared at the clipboard with disgust. 'My sister and her bloody lists.'

'When is Anna getting back? And it's definitely fifty, by the way.' Jude pointed to the boxes when she looked confused.

'Of course it is. Just like on the list.' Rosa ticked something off, and scowled at it again. 'Mama says she and Leo should be back this afternoon. With a full report of the catering staff that Valentina's flying in from Barcelona.' Perhaps her sister's imminent return explained Rosa's bad mood.

'This is going to be quite the wedding, huh?'

Jude opened the first box to find string after string of fairy lights, all neatly wrapped around pieces of card. The next box revealed larger lanterns to house candles, and the one after that the candles themselves.

'Is Valentina expecting some sort of power cut?' he asked, motioning towards the boxes.

Rosa laughed. 'Sort of. She wants a very traditional Spanish wedding, apparently—which means it doesn't start until the evening and it goes on all night long. And since it's all taking place outside...'

'Hence the candles.'

'Exactly.'

Rosa perched herself on the edge of the nearest box, sitting gingerly until she was certain it could take her weight. She'd pushed her sunglasses onto the top of her head, and her usual heavy plait hung over her shoulder. Jude couldn't help but watch her. What was it about her that drew his eye, even after everything? Even now he knew the risk of getting caught up in Rosa again?

She was beautiful, of course. Maybe even more beautiful than she'd been three years ago. She'd been fresher then, he supposed, but there was a new worldliness about her now that he liked.

The tension he'd noticed on the first day was still there, tight in the lines of her shoulders and her mouth, for all that she kicked her feet casually back and forth. She chewed a pencil as she stared down at her clipboard.

'Okay, so as far as I can tell, this is what's happening. The bridal party arrive on the Wednesday, for general wedding prep and whatever it is bridesmaids do before a wedding.'

'Drink, mostly, I think,' Jude said. 'Have you never been a bridesmaid?'

Rosa looked at him as if he were crazy. 'Aren't they supposed to organise things and commit to being in the country on the right day and stuff? Who on earth would ask me to do that?'

'Good point,' he allowed. Rosa wasn't the woman you went to for commitment. He had the heartbreak to prove it.

'Anyway, the groom and his family and

groomsmen arrive on Friday night, then the wedding is on the Saturday evening, so that whole day will probably be pretty hellish with last-minute traumas. If you wanted to run, I'd suggest you do it then.'

She was watching him from under her lashes, Jude realised. Waiting to see what his reaction to the idea of leaving was.

Did that mean she wanted him to stay? What had she said last night? *Some are worth experiencing twice.* Well. If that wasn't a hint…

'I'm not going anywhere,' he said, cursing himself a little as he did so. What was he doing, promising to stay for the woman who'd been running from him for three years?

'Want to stay and see the ex-girlfriend, huh?' Rosa asked, and Jude realised he'd actually forgotten for a moment that staying would mean seeing Sylvie.

'Not really.' Especially since thinking about her still made his blood boil.

'You said it was a bad breakup?'

'She fabricated stories about me to sell for the stupid kiss-and-tell book about me.' Of course, the made-up ones were easier to laugh off than the true, private ones she'd also sold. The ones where she'd talked about Gareth, and his remorse and guilt over his death. The broken promise. Those were the ones that hurt the most.

Gareth was no one's business except his.

'*The Naked Truth* thing?' Rosa winced. 'Ouch.'

'Yeah. The book came out this week.'

'Which is why you decided to be on a remote Spanish island at the time.'

'Exactly.'

'Except now your fantastically twisted love life is following you here,' Rosa commented.

Jude shot her a look. 'In more ways than one.'

'Well, you said you wanted closure.' Jumping down from the box she was sitting on, Rosa busied herself with sorting through a box full of orders of service and menus and such, sending them flying into haphazard piles on the other boxes. Jude foresaw a lot of resorting them in his future.

A figure appeared across the courtyard: Anna. Rosa's sister picked her way carefully past the reflecting pool towards them.

'Looks like you have some closure coming your way, too,' Jude said, nodding towards her.

Rosa spun round, then froze as she spotted Anna. The tension that had been hidden under casual, forced relaxation was suddenly obvious to all—but only for a moment. As Jude watched he could see Rosa purposefully relaxing her shoulders, her arms, as Anna grew closer. She took a few lazy steps towards her sister, then hopped up to sit on the large wooden table Sancia used for breakfasts, leaning back on her hands and waiting, letting Anna come the rest of the way to her.

Jude busied himself with the boxes, hoping it wasn't too obvious that he was eavesdropping.

They didn't hug. That was the first thing he noticed as the sisters greeted each other. What had Rosa said? That it had been three years since they'd last spoken.

He wondered if it was a coincidence that her last conversation with Anna must have been around the same time as she left him. Or was there more to the story than she'd told him before?

'You made it back, then,' Rosa said. 'I thought you might decide to just stay in Barcelona with this Leo I've heard so much about from Mama.'

'Not really my style, abandoning the family when they need me.' Anna's tone was mild, but Jude could hear a bite behind it.

'Right.' Rosa heard it, too, judging by the tightness of her reply. 'Mama gave me my chore list, by the way.'

'Good. Any problems?'

'Other than the fact I'd be much more use to Mama out on the island, dealing with stuff, than stuck going through lists of bungalow allocations and boxes of fairy lights.'

Anna looked past her and her gaze alighted on Jude, who looked away quickly. He did *not* want to get drawn into a sibling squabble. It was the only advantage he'd found to being an only child—and besides, bandmate squabbles were bad enough for him.

'Looks like you've found someone to palm some of the work off onto already, anyway,' Anna said, drily. 'Why am I not surprised?'

'Well, since you were off gallivanting with your Latin lover, I had to work with what I had.' Jude hadn't expected Rosa to go into the details of their complicated history, but hearing himself resigned to leftover help stung a little all the same.

'As long as it all gets done.' Anna turned away. 'Let me know if you can't manage any of it.' She tossed the words back over her shoulder as she walked away, and Jude saw Rosa's hands clench up into fists before they relaxed again.

'You okay?' he asked softly, once they were alone again.

Rosa spun round so fast he wondered if she'd forgotten he was there. Again.

'I'm fine.' Her clipped words said otherwise, but Jude didn't call her on it. Not yet, anyway. 'Come on. Leave this. We're going sailing.'

CHAPTER SIX

ROSA DIDN'T WAIT for Jude as she stormed down to the jetty. He'd catch her up if he wanted to come with her, and if he didn't she'd go alone.

So, it seemed that regular sex with a man Sancia had described as a hunky pirate hadn't mellowed Anna out any—which probably meant nothing could. She was still the big sister who thought she could run her life, who would always highlight her perceived mistakes and ignore her successes. Rosa didn't know why she'd imagined for a moment that three years apart would have changed anything.

The hardest part was, even now Rosa could see that eighteen-year-old Anna had only been trying to hold the family together after Mama left, it seemed that twenty-eight-year-old Anna still thought Rosa was the sixteen-year-old little sister she'd got used to bossing about. She still didn't trust her to take care of anything herself, not really. She had to control and manage everything, because only *Anna* could get it right.

Of course, some of that might be more to do with their argument three years ago…

Rosa shook her head. She wasn't thinking about that now.

The small boats the resort kept for guests to borrow to sail over to the mainland were all neatly tied up along the jetty, each looking freshly scrubbed and cleaned—which made Rosa scowl even more. Just extra evidence of all St Anna's hard work.

She squeezed her eyes tight and tried to get a grip on her temper. She was better than this. Older and if not wiser, at least more rational. She'd seen sights all over the world that others couldn't imagine, highlighted horrific situations to the public, and uncovered forgotten treasures with her work. She was *not* going to let herself get all riled up by her sister's martyr complex. That was just one of many things she'd decided to break free from when she'd left Britain, three years before.

The other main thing she'd broken free from caught her up pretty quickly, standing beside her as they stared at the boats.

'So, where are we going?' Jude asked, and Rosa realised that you couldn't leave everything behind, every time.

Sometimes you had to stand and face them.

But not Anna. Not today.

'The mainland,' she said, choosing a dinghy and starting to prep it to sail. 'There's a little seaside village, Cala del Mar, just across the way. It has the best tapas outside of Barcelona. Also, wine.'

'Then let's go,' Jude said, stepping aboard.

He let her get a little way away from the island before he started asking questions, which she appreciated.

'So, you and Anna. Any more you wanted to tell me about that?'

'Not really.' Mostly all she wanted to do was get away from the island for a while. Even a few days there had left her feeling claustrophobic, in a way living in a tent in a war zone or an unexplored rainforest never did.

'Because I realised something. If it's been three years since you last spoke to her, that must have been around the same time I last saw you.'

He was fishing. Suddenly Rosa regretted bringing Jude along. She'd hoped they were done talking about their past relationship, now she'd given him the closure he'd asked for, but apparently he wanted more.

'It was at my Grandfather's funeral, actually.' The mention of death usually shut people up.

Not Jude. 'A difficult, emotional time for you, then.'

Sighing, Rosa turned to face him. He lounged, pale and beautiful, against the back of the boat. His sharp cheekbones and brooding eyes that looked so perfect on album covers looked oddly out of place here on the water, as if he were a being from another world.

In a way, he was, she supposed. The world of celebrity, a million miles away from La Isla Marina, before this week. Now it looked as if it was going to be packed with them.

Hopefully none of the others would be so interested in her past.

'Look, why don't you just ask whatever it is you want to know?' Rip the plaster off and get it over with, that was her way of dealing with difficult things. Anna, as always, disagreed, most of the time.

'I just thought you might like to talk about it,' Jude said, mildly. 'I mean, whatever that last conversation was, it was clearly a corker.'

It had been. Fireworks and hateful words and dramatics all together. The culmination of seven years of frustration and lack of understanding. Of Anna never listening to Rosa's feelings, Anna always knowing best and Rosa always screwing up.

Rosa sank down to sit on the little bench at the

front of the boat, where she could keep steering, but slowed them to an almost stop so they just bobbed in the water. She needed her full attention for this conversation.

Maybe it would help to talk about it. If she could explain her side of the story, and have someone understand, maybe she'd stop feeling so damn guilty about it.

'Like I said, Anna and I had both come to the island for our *abuelo*'s funeral. Anna was fretting about leaving Dad home alone, which was ridiculous, because he's a grown, intelligent man who should be able to take care of himself.'

'But she thinks he can't?' Jude asked.

'Apparently. But it seems to me that if he can run his department, organise his research and make a career as a semi-famous Oxford academic, then he is perfectly capable of arranging his own meals and remembering to take his pills.'

'Pills?'

Rosa waved a hand. 'A preventative measure. He has a heart condition—has had it for years—so he has to take a few tablets to keep it under control.'

'And Anna makes sure he does?'

'Well, yes. Because she's St Anna and she wants to have everyone rely on her and say how wonderful she is.'

Jude tilted his head as he watched her, and Rosa looked away. She didn't like that knowing look in his eye. 'Do you really believe that?'

'No,' Rosa admitted, talking down to the bottom of the boat. 'I don't. But I think she's got so used to controlling everyone and everything she doesn't know how to stop. And I think Dad takes advantage of that. He likes having her to deal with all the boring things he doesn't want to have to think about—like how food gets in the cupboard, or how the house gets clean. He likes having his pills waiting for him by his breakfast plate in the morning, so he can pretend they're just vitamins and that he's fine. He likes Anna looking after him because it means he doesn't have to look after himself. You know, his cardiologist told him four years ago that if he changed his diet, exercised more and started cutting down his hours at work, he might be able to reduce the amount of medication he's on. But he wouldn't do it. Anna managed to sneak in some more healthy meals—although he still eats nothing but red meat and red wine when he dines at the college, I'm sure. And she bullies him into taking a walk now and then. But he won't even *talk* about retiring.'

'I've only known your father a week or so, but from playing Scrabble with him I can confirm that he is a very stubborn man.' Jude shifted, leaning forward with his elbows resting on his knees as he looked at her. 'So you were mad with Anna for letting your dad take advantage of her?'

'Sort of.' Rosa looked out over the water, back towards La Isla Marina, and thought of the real reason Anna hated her.

'Something else happened,' Jude guessed.

'Yeah.' Taking a deep breath, Rosa let herself remember that horrible night. 'She'd been offered a visiting professorship at Harvard, just for the semester, starting the term after the funeral. She wanted to take it, of course, but she—' She cut herself off.

'She didn't want to leave your dad alone,' Jude said. Rosa nodded. 'She asked you to stay with him?'

'She said that if I was there to take care of him, she'd feel like she could go. And it just made me so mad—not that she wanted me to stay home, but that she was putting her whole life on hold for a man who just saw her as a combination of nursemaid, housekeeper, chef and occasional replacement for the wife who'd left him at college functions. He always said how proud he was of her career, but he was holding her back—by not taking responsibility for his own health and well-being.'

A niggling whisper in the back of her brain reminded Rosa that their father had been abandoned when Sancia left, too. That he'd been trying to cope, just as Anna had, just as she had. That he'd wanted to keep the family he had left close.

But that wasn't enough of an excuse for stifling Anna's whole life, was it?

'What did you say?'

'I told her that she should go anyway. That I couldn't stay with him—let's be honest, I wouldn't have been any good at doing all the stuff Anna did for him, anyhow.' Rosa knew her limitations. If she'd been forced to babysit her father for three months, one of them would have moved out within the first few days for sure. 'But that she shouldn't feel tied down by him. He's a grown man, not her responsibility any more.'

'She didn't go to Harvard, did she?'

Rosa shook her head, deflating from her righteous indignation. 'No. She stayed there and put her life on hold for him, like always. And I...'

'Ran to the other side of the world to get away from me.'

'Not just you,' Rosa admitted, meeting his gaze for the first time since the conversation started. To her amazement, she saw understanding there, rather than judgement. 'Like you said, it was an emotional time.'

'It sounds it.' Cautiously—he obviously wasn't used to being on the water—Jude crossed the boat towards her, crouching in front of her and taking her hand. 'I can understand why Anna would be mad and disappointed, but that doesn't mean you were wrong. If anything, it seems to me like you were trying to help her.'

'Not very well, it seems.' She blinked, hard, to try and stop the prickling behind her eyes. She was *not* going to cry about this. Especially in front of Jude.

'Oh, I don't know,' Jude said, giving her a small smile. 'I mean, it might have taken her a while, but she came here, didn't she? She left Oxford to come and help out your mum.'

'Dragging Dad after her for the good of his health,' Rosa pointed out. 'But maybe you're right. It's a start.'

And maybe Leo could be the next step for Anna. She should find out some more about him. Make sure he wasn't just going to take over Anna's life in their father's place.

But for now... Rosa looked down at Jude. He had the same look Anna had sometimes—the tightness around the eyes and the tenseness of the shoulders that told her he was trying too hard for the wrong things. He'd never looked like that three years ago. Then he'd been all enthusiasm and excitement—and loose-limbed, bone-deep satisfaction in bed afterwards.

No. She wasn't thinking about that. She was thinking as a friend, not an ex-lover.

And as a friend, she could see that Jude needed to cut loose a bit. Maybe she was the one who could help him lighten up.

'You know, you're far too pale for this place. Come on. Let's go get tapas and wine and sit in the sunshine for a while.'

Cala del Mar was a perfect, sleepy seaside fishing village. Jude strolled along the seafront with Rosa at his side and wondered if he'd be happier somewhere like this, than in New York City. Rosa certainly seemed content enough—but he suspected that, like everything else in Rosa's life, would only last until she got bored.

And he had promises to keep. Music to make. And Gareth's memory to preserve, out there in the real world.

Fishing boats still bobbed out on the waves, under the slowly fading sunlight that sparkled and shone on the water. The air was warm around them and, for a moment, Jude could almost let himself believe that he was here with Rosa, celebrating their three-year anniversary or something—instead of as wary acquaintances working together on a celebrity wedding.

'The place I wanted to show you is up here,' Rosa said, leading him to a narrow flight of steep stone steps that wound up between the tiny painted cottages and shops into the heart of the village. The walls either side of the stairs were cold and damp, their location meaning they were permanently in shadow. Jude kept his gaze firmly on Rosa's swaying plait as they climbed, refusing to look lower, or let him think about all the things this evening wasn't.

It wasn't a date, however it felt. It wasn't even an opportunity. He'd learned that lesson too well the first time.

The tapas place Rosa led him to barely even qualified as a restaurant. It had two tables inside by the bar, and another three out on the balcony, looking out over the seafront. Rosa chatted happily in Spanish to the elderly man behind the bar, who welcomed her warmly, and moments later they were seated out at the best balcony table, olives, breads, oil, vinegar and a carafe of red wine between them.

Rosa filled up their glasses. 'Doesn't this feel better already?'

'Much.' It wasn't a lie, not exactly. It *did* feel wonderful to be relaxing in the sunshine with a beautiful woman, with good food and better wine. He just wished he could shake the feeling that it wasn't enough, just being with Rosa this way, unable to take her in his arms and kiss her whenever he wanted.

But then…the story she'd told him about her argument with Anna still pulsed around his head. And he couldn't help wondering, if she hadn't argued with her sister, might Rosa have come back to him? Had she felt that returning to him, to the tour, to his life, would be the same as Anna sticking with their father's life even though she wanted more?

It wouldn't have made any difference, in the long run, he supposed. Rosa there was as distracting as Rosa gone; he still might have missed the signs with Gareth. It was *his* obsession that was to blame there, not Rosa.

But if the argument with Anna *was* why she had left…maybe he could convince her that things were different, now.

Jude leant back in his chair and watched Rosa watch the sea. He didn't dream of for ever with her, not the way his younger self had. He knew she wasn't a for ever kind of girl. Rosa would never stay in one place long enough to be tied down by love—she was too full of life, a free spirit. He wouldn't *want* to contain her that way and make her unhappy.

And like it or not, his real life was waiting

for him back in New York, once the furore over the book had died down. He'd go back to the band, to making music he loved, and doing all the things the label expected him to do to keep The Swifts in the public eye and their music selling.

But right now, while they were both here together...could there be a chance for something more between them? An island fling, perhaps, with none of the expectations and hopes he'd placed on them before.

If he could convince Rosa that all he wanted was right now, maybe he could have her in his arms again.

And maybe that would be worth the potential pain of watching her walk away once more. At least this time, he knew it was coming, and could prepare himself for it.

He wasn't angry at her for leaving him, not any more. He understood, even if he didn't like it. But Jude was starting to think that the closure he needed to *truly* move on didn't come in words. It wasn't explanations he needed.

It was touch.

'It's hard to stay mad too long in a place like this, isn't it?' Rosa said, looking back from the sea.

'Yeah,' Jude agreed. 'It is.' Only he wasn't talking about her argument with Anna.

He was imagining how the next two weeks might cure him of that anger and resentment for good.

Rosa had been staring at the guest list so long it had given her a headache. Over the handful of days she and Jude had made good progress with all things organisational for the wedding, but the bungalow allocations were still causing her trouble. Every time she thought she had it sorted, she found another name, or another couple who couldn't be near someone else, or who needed something specific that the bungalow she'd assigned them didn't have. When she added in the constant phone calls from guests to add extra requirements to their bookings, she wanted to throw the stupid clipboard into the sea and head for the airport.

It was, quite frankly, an impossible task. One even Jude had given up on and disappeared off with his guitar after taking a call from his agent.

Rosa would be ready to admit defeat if doing so didn't mean telling Anna she wasn't up to the job.

And speaking of Anna…after her talk with Jude on the boat, Rosa had been doing a lot of thinking about her sister. And more specifically, about Anna and her new beau. Rosa had done some research, and what she'd learned hadn't made her any more comfortable with Anna's relationship. Leo di Marquez had *quite* the reputation—and it wasn't the good sort. International playboy, gambler and general debauched human being by all accounts, he was most definitely not Anna's usual type. In fact, she could only remember Anna dating anyone vaguely like that once before—and given how that had ended, Rosa didn't look forward to a repeat of the experience.

In the end, she realised she was going to have to talk to her sister. About Leo, and about the room bookings.

What the hell. She needed a walk anyway.

As it turned out, though, she didn't have to go far to find her sister—she was already in the villa reception area. Leaning against the office doorway, Rosa watched Anna staring out towards the courtyard, a soft smile on her face, and wished that she could just let Anna enjoy the fun and relaxation of no-strings sex with a gorgeous man. Except Anna didn't do casual, and the way things were going Rosa was pretty sure her sister was going to end up with a broken heart. Again.

'You're looking all doe-eyed. Does Señor Tall, Dark and Handsome have anything to do with that?' As an opening gambit, it wasn't great, but it got Anna's attention at least. She spun round and glared at Rosa.

Then she replaced the glare with an overly sweet smile. 'None of your business.'

Right. Of course.

'How's the paperwork?' Anna asked. 'Sorted out the wedding guests into rooms yet?'

Rosa's jaw clenched at the reminder. 'I don't understand why you're being so stubborn. You love spreadsheets and solving problems. I love being outside and fixing things. We should just swap…'

'If you'd hadn't arrived over two weeks late then you could have had your pick of jobs. As it was I had to get on and do what needed doing most. You keep going with the wedding planning and helping Mama with the office. It'll do you good to stretch yourself.'

Still trying to control things for my own good, huh, St Anna?

Rosa's good intentions faded away as her ire rose at the condemnation in Anna's voice. 'Of course you dropped everything and rushed straight here.'

'It's a good thing I did, look at what your *"stand back and let them make their own mistakes"* plan has achieved. This place was chaos…'

'Chaos until St Anna turned up and fixed it

all?' Like always. She had to be the saviour, didn't she?

'Yes. Actually.'

'Dragging Dad with you? Couldn't trust him on his own for a month?' God forbid that anyone be allowed to take control of their own lives for a change.

'Dad turned up on his own.' Anna folded her arms over her T-shirt. 'You do know he nearly died?' she said almost conversationally.

'What?' Rosa's chest tightened. Then she realised Anna had to be exaggerating. 'Nonsense, he looks fine.'

'He looks fine now. He looks fine because he has no stress outside work, his meals are prepared, he takes his pills, he gets reminded to take regular walks. Not because I'm a saint, not because I'm a martyr, but because someone has to do it—and no.' Anna raised her hand as Rosa tried to interrupt. 'Don't tell me he's an adult. I know that. I also know that when he wants to be he's the most organised man alive. But his health isn't a priority, work is. And he would forget, just like Mama forgot to take care of the basics here. So what do I do, Rosa? Swan off to Harvard and let him get ill and Mama sink? Is that your answer?'

Yes. Yes, it was. Because it might not be the perfect answer, but what else was there? How could Anna mortgage her life to their father when he couldn't be bothered to even look after himself?

'I don't understand.' She never had. It didn't make any *sense*. But Anna's words—*nearly died*—echoed through her head again and again. 'I was ten before I realised other families didn't get given their own individual holiday itineraries and checklists two weeks before they went on holiday, and most families didn't stock check their cupboards monthly. How can he not remember to take his pills?' He could, if he wanted to. It was just easier to let Anna do it. That was all. And until she left him to take care of himself, it always would be.

'Things changed after Mama left.' Anna blew a frustrated breath. 'You were still at home then, Rosa. I know how self-centred you are, but surely even you noticed?'

She just couldn't resist getting another jibe in there, could she? Another complaint about how Rosa wasn't as perfect as Anna, and never would be. Really, when you knew you could never live up to expectations, why even try?

'I know you got bossier and more self-righteous than ever. I know you refused to move into halls during term time, staying at home to prove what a good daughter you are. At least until you started seeing that guy, then suddenly we saw another side of Anna…until he dumped you, that is. Then you got even more boring than before.' Rosa ignored the pang of guilt in her chest. This wasn't how she'd meant this conversation to go. But somehow, whenever she was faced with Anna and her perfection, she just lost any cool rationality she'd ever possessed. Why did the people closest to you sometimes bring out your worst side?

'It's always lovely catching up with you, Rosa, but I have a lot to do. Good luck with those spreadsheets.' Anna turned away, and Rosa realised she'd missed her chance. She'd screwed it up again, just as she always did with her sister.

No. This time, she was going to give it one more try.

'I'm just worried about you, Anna,' she said, and her voice stopped Anna in her tracks. 'Leo di Marquez isn't the kind of man you're used to…'

'I'm more than capable of handling Leo, thank you,' Anna said, dismissively.

'I just don't want a repeat of the Sebastian situation. I mean, he was an utter idiot, and Leo doesn't appear to be quite so arrogant, or as sleazy, but he broke you, Anna. I don't want that to happen again.'

Was Anna crying? No. Rosa couldn't remember the last time she'd seen her sister do that.

'Sebastian didn't break me, Rosa. I did that all by myself.' And with that, Anna walked away, leaving Rosa alone with her clipboard, and the feeling she might have just made things worse between her and her sister.

'I didn't even know that was possible,' she muttered.

CHAPTER SEVEN

WITH ONE MORE day to go until Valentina and her bridal party arrived, it seemed that La Isla Marina was almost ready for its sudden brush with celebrity. Jude had to admit, the place was looking a lot better than when he'd arrived. And last time he'd checked, Rosa had *almost* finished the room allocations, which were proving more of a nightmare than either of them had predicted.

He was almost glad of his agent's call as an excuse to get away from helping for a while. Almost.

'What's up, Robyn?' he said, sauntering towards his bungalow and his guitar as he answered.

'When are you coming back?' Robyn asked, bluntly. 'With all the publicity about the book, we need you here, capitalising on that.'

'I think people are perfectly capable of talking about me without me actually being there to hear it.' God knew, they managed it often enough normally.

'Look, Jude, I know you're not happy about some of the things they say in the book—'

'I'm not happy that the book exists at all.'

'But it does. You can't unprint it now, or stop people from reading it.'

'I could sue for defamation,' Jude suggested, although he knew he wouldn't.

'Do you really want to have to go to court and prove which of those stories are lies?' Robyn asked, gently.

Jude sighed. 'No.' Because in doing so, he'd only be confirming that all the others were true. And all the worst ones were, unfortunately. 'I just wish they hadn't written so much about Gareth.' And how Jude had let him down.

His mind flashed back to that day in the hospital, almost a year to the day before Gareth died.

He could still hear Gareth's raspy, exhausted voice saying, *'I know. I know I have to stop. But I need help.'*

And his own reply. *'I'll help. I'll be there every day, reminding you of everything you have to live for. Keeping you out of trouble just like I've always done. I promise.'*

It wasn't the idea of the whole world knowing how he'd betrayed his best friend's trust that upset him. It was seeing that betrayal in black-and-white and knowing that there was nothing he could do about it. No way to change the past, however much he wished he could.

Somehow, the book made it all real, all over again. Just like seeing Rosa again transported him back three years to a time when the only place he could be happy was in her arms.

'I never met him, but from what you've told me about him? Gareth would have loved being the centre of attention in a bestselling book.' Robyn had only become their agent after The Swifts hit the big time. But Gareth was part of the band's legacy, its history, and it had been important to Jude that she know all about him.

Apparently she'd got a pretty good handle on him, after all. 'He'd have been mad the book wasn't all about him.'

'Do you wish it was?'

'If it meant he was still here with us? Definitely. As it is…no.' Bad enough to have his memory raked over the coals in a few early chapters of this book. But a whole book trashing Gareth's memory? Jude couldn't have lived with that.

'Jude…these books don't mean anything. Not really. You know that.'

'I know. I just… Sylvie gave them a lot of those stories, you know?'

'I suspected.' Jude was pretty sure Robyn was wincing on the other end of the line. 'She knows how to play the game, that one.'

'Yeah.' Rosa didn't. Rosa had no idea of the rules of any game but her own. 'Look, Robyn, I've got to go. But if you get lucky, you might get some photos of me online sooner rather than later.'

'Really?' Robyn perked up at the idea. 'Why? Where are you? And who are you with, more to the point? Because if it's a woman, a nice, juicy, romantic scandal would definitely distract from the book...'

Jude laughed, and thought of Rosa. 'I'll see what I can do.'

But not for the publicity. For himself.

To celebrate actually managing to get ready on time, beating all the odds, Sancia had insisted on a family dinner that night—a proper, five-course banquet with matching wines, by all accounts. Jude wasn't exactly sure what he'd done to make Sancia think he was family and issue an invite, but he wasn't about to turn down the spectacular catering at the villa, either. Besides, Rosa would be there, and that was enough for him.

Things had been so busy since their trip to the mainland that the time simply hadn't been right for him to propose any sort of rekindling of their relationship to her. But now, with everything almost sorted, perhaps tonight could be the night. And just because they hadn't been physically intimate, that didn't mean they hadn't grown closer. Working together, seeing each other every day, talking about their lives and families—sometimes, Jude felt closer to Rosa now than when they'd been in the midst of their passionate affair three years ago.

He'd been at a bit of a loss for a hostess gift for the dinner, since Sancia technically already owned everything on the island, but he had brought his guitar, in case he could offer some background entertainment later. He'd been listening to a lot of classical Spanish guitar music since he arrived, playing around with some ideas on the theme, coming up with new threads and melodies that might one day become actual songs. It was kind of exciting, to be working on new music again—just him, messing around with tunes that appealed to him, rather than arguing with the rest of the band about what direction The Swifts should be moving in, musically, and what fitted best with their brand.

Jude didn't want to be a brand. He wanted to be a musician. And here, on La Isla Marina, he almost felt as if he could be, again.

So, anyway, he was looking forward to dinner that evening. At least, until he sat down at the table.

Professor Gray sat at the head of the table on one end, with Sancia at the other. Jude found himself sitting opposite Rosa, either side of her father, with Anna on his left, and Leo opposite her. Straight away, he could feel the tension strung out across the table like the fairy lights hanging overhead.

Rosa didn't look at her dad, he realised. In fact, he wasn't sure he'd seen her talk to him at all since the day she first arrived on the island. He'd been so focussed on her relationship with her sister, he hadn't noticed the fissure between her and her father. But from everything she'd said about him, Jude wasn't really surprised. It was hard to imagine the buttoned-up and structured Professor Gray appreciating the wildness of his younger daughter.

Unfortunately, the situation with Anna didn't look much brighter, given the way she and Rosa were both avoiding each other's gaze.

Anna and Leo spoke quietly across the table, intimate and happy, as they worked their way through the first course. Jude tried to strike up a conversation with Rosa, of the sort they'd been having more often of late, but she was distracted, and he couldn't seem to connect with her. Eventually, he gave up and chatted amiably with Professor Gray about his latest research. As ever, the professor was happy enough to carry on a monologue for most of the meal, so it wasn't as if Jude needed to contribute a lot.

'So, Leo,' Rosa said suddenly, cutting across the other chatter at the table. 'Why *are* you helping out so much for Valentina's wedding?'

The hint was there, Jude realised, behind the question—the idea that Leo must have a prior relationship with the star, or something. What was Rosa trying to do? Drive a wedge between Anna and Leo? He knew she was concerned about Leo's reputation, but watching them together Jude couldn't help but think that Rosa had judged this one wrong. He'd never seen a man so obviously in love as Leo di Marquez.

'Valentina is Leo's half-sister,' Anna said, after a quick glance across the table to confirm it was okay to do so.

Rosa's eyebrows rose up towards her hairline. 'I didn't know she had a brother.'

'Not many people do.' Leo sounded obviously uncomfortable with the situation. 'We didn't grow up together.'

'Do you think she'll be pleased with the island?' Jude asked, trying to get back onto safer topics.

Leo's expression warmed. 'I think she'll love it,' he said, smiling across at Anna as he spoke.

'Oh, it's so lovely to have all my family here once more,' Sancia said, beaming around the table. 'And to see both my girls so happy with their men.'

Jude's gaze flew to Rosa, who stared back, wide-eyed and panicked.

'Oh, we're not—' she started.

As Jude said, 'Actually, we're just friends.'

Sancia didn't reply, just smiled knowingly at them both.

Rosa was silent for the rest of the meal. Jude tried to concentrate on his conversation with Professor Gray, but by the time they finished dessert he wasn't sure he could have said for certain what they'd even been talking about. His attention kept being drawn across the table, to where Rosa sat quiet and subdued, sneaking glances at her sister from time to time.

When Sancia motioned for the coffee and liqueurs to be brought out, Rosa pushed her chair back from the table, mumbling some sort of excuse. Jude watched her go, wondering if he should follow, or if he'd only make things worse. But when he glanced up the table, he saw Sancia staring at him, eyebrows raised, and realised that Rosa's mother, at least, had a clear idea of what was best for her.

'Take these,' she murmured as he passed, and Jude accepted the two wine glasses and the rest of the bottle of red gratefully. He'd take whatever help he could get in trying to understand Rosa.

He found her out on the back veranda, looking out over the far side of the island towards the sea.

'Thinking about escaping?' he asked, handing her a full glass of wine, and placing the bottle on the nearest table.

'Always,' Rosa replied, and Jude thought it might have been the most honest thing she'd ever said to him.

'I'd like it if you'd stay, for a while at least.' He perched on the edge of the table, looking up at her in the shadows of the night. Overhead, the moon was almost full, and he could make out every contour of her face, every uncertainty in her eyes, even in the darkness.

'You know they all think we're sleeping together,' Rosa said, bluntly. 'Mama is probably planning some sort of huge double wedding for me and Anna, even though we're not a couple and Leo is going to walk out and break Anna's heart any day now.'

'You don't know that for sure,' Jude said. Although, given what he'd heard about Leo's reputation, he could see Rosa's point.

'Ah, but you see, I do.' Rosa's smile was sad. 'Leo and me, we're cut from the same cloth, I reckon. Not made to stay. We have to keep moving to keep living.'

'Like sharks,' Jude said, absently remembering a nature documentary he'd watched on some flight to a gig, somewhere or another.

'I bite, too,' Rosa joked.

'I remember.' The words were out before he could even think about them, and instantly the image they conjured up heated his blood.

No wonder her family thought they were together. If his gaze was half as heated as the one she had trained on him, then they must look as if they'd been lovers for years.

Rosa licked her lips, and Jude felt the pressure building inside him. He had to say something. Do something.

He had to have her again—even if she left him tomorrow.

Just one more night with her, that was all he needed.

God, he sounded like Gareth, at the end.

Just one more hit. I'll quit tomorrow, Jude, I promise. Just one more. One more for the road...'

Was he every bit an addict as his friend had been? And while his addiction might not be so deadly, could Jude really say it wouldn't destroy him, all the same?

But then Rosa said, 'Let's go for a swim,' and he stopped thinking altogether.

If he was an addict, maybe he didn't care any more. He needed one more night with Rosa Gray.

She didn't have to ask Jude twice. Whether he'd read her mind, or their mutual lust had just taken over his brain as it seemed to have taken over hers, he abandoned the wine and followed her down to the beach without question.

Rosa didn't think too much about what she was doing. Overthinking wasn't her style—she was more of an impulse person. She went with what her instincts told her were right and, if it went wrong, well, at least she'd been true to herself.

Tonight, she felt as if she was being true to an impulse she'd been denying for three long years. And the relief of it was almost overwhelming.

'There's a cove, just around here,' she said, picking her way over the rocks and out of sight of the villa. She really didn't want any of her family members coming looking for them tonight.

Tonight was about her and Jude. Not them.

She could feel him behind her, feel the heat of him jumping the inch or two of space between them.

Maybe this was inevitable. Maybe, from the moment she'd first seen him sitting there in the courtyard, as if he'd been waiting for her, they'd been leading to this.

Maybe this was the *real* closure Jude had been looking for.

One more night together. Maybe that was what they both needed to be able to move on.

All Rosa knew was she couldn't have sat at that dinner table any longer, with everyone playing perfect happy families, when she knew what a lie it was. They were all pretending that they were settled, stable, that this was how things would be for ever. But none of that was true. Her parents hadn't been together in ten years— and if she knew them at all, she doubted they'd even talked about why Sancia had left, all those years ago. Nothing had been resolved. Anna and Leo weren't going to live happily ever after, whatever fairy tales Anna was telling herself. Things would get hard and Leo would run, and so would Sancia.

And as for Rosa and Jude…they weren't even ever a couple. Not really.

And they weren't about to start now.

But there was something between them, that much was true. And if she had to stay here on the island and witness all this hypocrisy, at least she could get to explore the fun side of it, too.

Jude knew who she was now. He wouldn't be fooled into thinking she'd stay, this time.

This time, it was all about transient fun. About freedom and enjoyment and letting the wildness inside loose again.

And what was more wild and free than swimming naked in the ocean?

The cove was just as she remembered: tucked away at the back of the island, protected by rocks and cliffs on either side, but with a small crescent-shaped beach in the centre. Rosa hopped down onto the sand, the sea already calling her. Even in the dark, it glistened in the moonlight, open and wide and free.

Without pausing in her stride, Rosa pulled off her top, and heard a sharp intake of breath behind her.

She spun to face Jude, still walking backwards as she fumbled with the clasp of her bra, letting it fall to the sand at her feet.

'Is this safe?' Jude asked, his eyes nowhere near her face.

'Do you care?' she asked, grinning.

'No.'

Rosa pushed her skirt and her underwear down her legs at the same time, stepped out of them and ran for the water, knowing that Jude wouldn't be far behind her.

The sea flowed cool and fresh against her hot skin, the salt stinging and sharp. Rosa welcomed every sensation—the rocks and sand under her feet, the water lapping against her, the breeze that blew loose strands of hair around her face. She stayed, treading water, just far enough out to be out of her depth—just where she liked to be—and watched Jude as he stripped off on the shoreline.

His skin was pale in the moonlight, his hair so dark it was almost lost in the night. But his body…oh, there were those lean, strong muscles she remembered. Those powerful legs, those well-defined arms and abs. That trail of hair that led down his body…

She remembered every inch of him. And she wanted him again.

He didn't flinch as he stepped into the cool water; she admired that. Throwing him a reckless grin, she flipped in the waves, diving underneath and kicking hard until she was further out. Let him chase her, the way he never had when she left.

That thought tugged at something in her mind, but she pushed it away to worry about another day.

Right now, all she wanted to do was enjoy the water on her skin, and Jude—when he caught her.

It didn't take him long.

She surfaced, a short way from where she'd watched him enter the water, and already she could see his powerful arms scything through the waves, propelling him towards her. He was barely even out of breath when he reached her side, treading water next to her as his arms reached out to slide around her waist.

His hands glided over her skin, under the water, pulling her close against him. Her whole body vibrated with the surety that this was right. This was meant to be. Here, now, like this. Wild and free and passionate—just the way they'd been together three years before.

She knew he was going to kiss her before his lips even lowered to hers, knew the surge of need that would pulse through her at the feel of his mouth, his tongue.

'Rosa.' He murmured her name like a wish.

'Let's take this to the shallows,' she whispered, pushing away from him and swimming for the shore.

Soon, Jude Alexander would make love to her again. And then maybe the island would feel like where she belonged.

CHAPTER EIGHT

LATER—MUCH LATER—they lay in each other's arms on the beach and watched the stars overhead.

'Planning on running away yet?' Jude asked, pressing a kiss to Rosa's bare shoulder. Her olive skin felt smooth and soft under his lips, the clothes they'd abandoned on the beach protecting them both from the sand.

'Not *just* yet.' Rosa stretched out against him, her body pressing closer to his. 'I might need to do that a few more times first.'

A few more times. At least he had some idea of a timetable now, then.

So much for one more night. He should have known—having Rosa again only made him want her more. For as long as they had together, anyway.

'You don't need to, this time,' he said, trying to keep his tone light. He wasn't usually one for serious relationship talk straight after sex, but if he'd learned one thing about Rosa it was that if he didn't get in there fast she'd be gone before he ever got the chance to say anything. 'Run, I mean.'

'Oh?' Propping herself up on one elbow, Rosa looked down at him, her damp hair curling around her face where it had escaped her braid. 'Why's that?'

'Because I know the deal, this time.' Jude swept his hands up her back, under her heavy plait, enjoying the opportunity to explore all that beautiful skin. 'No strings, no expectations, right? Just you and me, enjoying the time we have together on the island.'

'A fling,' Rosa said, her mouth twitching up into a lopsided smile. 'An island romance.'

'Exactly.'

'Sounds perfect.'

She kissed him again, then, and Jude forgot for a moment how much it had hurt when she left, before.

Not this time, though. This time, he was prepared, he knew what he was getting into. He could steel his heart against falling for Rosa Gray all over again. Right?

'Besides,' Rosa said, sliding down to nestle in the crook of his arm again, her head resting against his shoulder, 'you'll be running back to New York again yourself any time soon, right?'

'Yeah.' New York. The city for dreamers. The place he'd wanted to get to his whole life. Except now, it felt like the last place he belonged. Especially without Gareth there to share it.

'There's a considerable lack of enthusiasm in that "yeah",' Rosa pointed out. 'Want to talk about it?'

Jude sighed. Did he? Maybe it would help. And Rosa... Rosa was one of the few people, other than his bandmates, who knew him well enough to understand. She knew what he'd been looking for in his music, in his career. What he'd hoped for from fame.

She might understand why he was disappointed with what he'd found instead.

'I am aware that this could be considered as being ungrateful,' he said, as an opening disclaimer.

Rosa laughed. 'Remember who you're talking to here. Just ask Anna how well I know ungrateful.'

Jude hugged her a little closer to him. Whatever had been bothering her at dinner still rankled, it seemed. He'd hoped that the last hour or so of being naked in his arms might have cured it. Maybe he'd have to try again...

'You've stopped talking,' Rosa pointed out as he started kissing along her hairline again.

Talking. Right.

Jude sighed, and dropped his head back down to his shirt on the sand. 'Do you remember, on the tour bus, how we talked about music and fame and everything that went with it?'

'Yes.' He hadn't expected her to sound so definite. It was three years ago, after all. 'I remember it all, Jude.'

His heart contracted at that. He'd always assumed she'd cared less than him, to be able to leave so easily. But there was something in her voice, a weight he hadn't expected. Maybe he'd misjudged her.

Except that she'd still left. Nothing she said now could change that simple fact.

'I thought that making music and getting paid for it would be enough. Gareth always wanted more, of course—he was the one who wanted the stardom, really. Wanted to show them all. He needed the riches and the success and his face in every magazine... I just wanted... I wanted to create something new and share it with the world. It was as simple—and as naive—as that.' He almost pitied the younger man he'd been. The Jude who'd thought that music was enough and that Rosa would stay. That Gareth's star, burning so bright, wouldn't consume him in the end. That he could hold the world together the way he wanted it through sheer force of will.

Thank goodness he grew up.

'And now?'

'Now I know it doesn't work like that.'

Rosa pressed a kiss to his bare chest, right above his heart. 'Maybe it should.'

He huffed a laugh. 'Maybe. But instead… I shouldn't complain. I get to do a job others would do for free and I get paid obscene amounts of money for it. And normally I'm fine with what that means.'

'What *does* it mean?'

'It means…' Jude sighed as he trailed off. 'It means being Jude Alexander the brand, rather than the man. It means deciding if the songs I write fit the band's direction, rather than if I like them. It means considering the label, the fans, the advertisers before the music.' It meant being the person Gareth had always been, the one who thought about how to be a success first.

'Putting them all before yourself,' Rosa added.

'Sometimes.' The truth was, he'd got so used to being led to the decisions others wanted him to make, to automatically defaulting to the best business decision, he wasn't sure if he even knew what *he* wanted any more.

Except for one thing: he knew he wanted to live Gareth's dreams for him, now he was no longer there to live them himself.

That was what mattered. Gareth's memory, and the music.

He owed Gareth that much, at least, if that was all there was left to give.

'And then there was the book…' Rosa lifted her head to look him in the eye. 'I guess that didn't go down well with the label?'

Jude laughed. 'The opposite, actually. They loved it. It made me sound like a real rock star—affairs and parties and wild behaviour. Add in Gareth's addiction and everything that came after and it was exactly what people imagine rock-star life to be.'

'Was it true, though?'

'Some of it,' Jude admitted. 'Some of it was exaggerated, and some just plain fantasy. But it didn't seem to matter. The publicity around it, even before it came out, was enough to bump our latest album a bit further up the charts.'

'All publicity is good publicity, huh?'

'It seems so.'

'Not for you, though.'

Jude closed his eyes, shutting out the stars above. 'No.'

'Tell me?' He felt Rosa inch closer, her leg over his, her arm around his waist. She was wrapping herself around him like a protective blanket, as if she could ward off the dark or the bad memories or both. He smiled, involuntarily.

For someone who never stayed, while she was there, Rosa could make a man feel as if he were the whole world.

Fame had done that for a while, too. He'd felt important, the big man in the city, just as he and Gareth had dreamed when they were poor schoolboys with no future. And yes, he'd taken advantage of it. He'd done things he looked back on and winced. He'd treated people badly, tossed his fame around like confetti.

But that wasn't who he really was. He knew that, now, even if the readers of *Jude: The Naked Truth* never would.

'Imagine someone printed a book that detailed every screw-up you'd ever made, every bad choice, every awful day, every time you were an idiot or just plain rude. And now imagine that anyone who ever thought anything of you is going to read that.'

Rosa squeezed him a little tighter around the middle. 'I don't think there's a book long enough for all my screw-ups.'

'Mine appears to be pretty lengthy, too.' He sighed. 'The worst part was realising all the people I'd trusted who must have contributed to it. There are stories in there that only a few people knew. The author—who has never actually met me, by the way—couldn't have got them from anyone else.'

Suddenly the warmth of Rosa's body next to him was gone, and when he opened his eyes she was sitting up over him, her arm across her bare breasts. 'I'm not in there, right? Because, Jude—you know I didn't talk to anyone, don't you? I wouldn't—'

'You're not in the book,' Jude told her, grabbing her hands and pulling her back down to him. 'You…that's one screw-up I know you'd never make.' She'd break his heart, leave without a backward glance, but Rosa would never sell him out. He'd doubted, for a time, but now he was sure.

'Okay. Good.'

'My ex-girlfriend, however, had no such restraint.' And that still hurt. Yes, maybe he and Sylvie were never going to make it long-term, but still.

Rosa winced on his behalf. 'You said she sold her story after you broke up?'

'Worse. She sold it when we were still dating. I only found out *after* we broke up.'

'Ouch.'

'Yeah.'

'So…not really looking forward to seeing her tomorrow, then?' Rosa asked.

Jude hauled her further up his body so he could kiss her thoroughly. 'I'm really not thinking about my ex-girlfriend right now.'

'Mmm, good.' Rosa returned the kiss. Then she pulled a little way away, her gaze uncertain. As if she didn't want to know the answer to the question she was about to ask. 'Jude. What happened with Gareth?'

In a way, he was surprised she'd waited so long to ask. Gareth had adored Rosa, and she'd returned the feeling. Jude had loved that—seeing the two people who knew him best getting along so well. Of course she needed to know the full, awful story.

But her question still hit him in the gut. Was he afraid of his own guilt, or passing some of it on to her by association? He wasn't sure any more.

'You read the newspaper reports, I'm sure,' Jude said, no emotion in his voice. 'They were very…comprehensive.'

Every single detail, spelled out in black-and-white print. They'd only just started making a noise on the scene, but Gareth was a big part of that noise. He was the one people had heard of, the one they wanted to see perform, back then. Jude had just been the guitarist, the accompanying vocals, not the frontman.

Not while Gareth was there to sing for both of them.

And when he had gone…of course, he'd blazed out in the most sensational way he could. Gareth wouldn't have known any other way.

'I read…it was at the awards show, wasn't it?'

Their first awards show. Their first award—best up-and-coming band, as voted for by *Melody Magazine*. The first sign that they were getting where they needed to go.

'He wanted to celebrate, of course.' Jude swallowed around the lump in his throat.

'Gareth always did.' Rosa's smile was soft, and he knew she was remembering. 'He celebrated everything, didn't he? A birthday, a gig, a sunrise. Hell, he threw a party the night we first slept together.'

'He said me getting laid was a rare enough occurrence that it deserved marking,' Jude said, drily.

'So. He went to the after-party to celebrate?' Rosa asked.

Jude's laugh felt so sharp it hurt his throat. 'Oh, Gareth couldn't wait that long. He went straight to the gents and shot up there. With a little celebratory extra, of course.' And he should have gone with him, been with him to stop him, to keep an eye on him. Should have stopped it before it even got that far. As he'd promised. 'It was that extra that killed him.'

But he'd been at the bar, drinking away the knowledge that Rosa wasn't coming back to him.

'They found him an hour or so later, when someone got suspicious about why the stall was still locked.' That was the worst part. It hadn't even been Jude who realised he was missing. He'd just assumed he was off chatting up some woman, or partying with his other friends. He hadn't even realised Gareth was using again, he'd been so self-absorbed. 'He was already gone, but they called the ambulance anyway. The paramedics stormed through just as they were announcing the winner of Artist of the Year.'

And so, of course, it made all the papers. Every gossip rag and website had the story—and the photos. Jude, pale and gaunt beside the stretcher, holding onto the closest thing to a brother he'd ever had.

'I made him a promise, you know,' he said, squeezing his eyes tight shut. 'A year before he died, he had a close call. Ended up in hospital after an accidental overdose, and it was touch-and-go for a while. When he woke up, I swore to him that I wouldn't let it happen again. I would keep him clean and straight and away from temptation. I'd be the angel on his shoulder. I promised I'd keep him alive. He had so much to live for…'

'Jude.' Rosa's cool hand pressed against his face, followed by her kiss. 'That wasn't a promise you could keep. No one could keep that promise. Gareth's addiction…you couldn't beat it with words.'

'Why not?' Jude cried out, into the night. 'Everything else in my life, it's all been words and music. That's what I have. I've fought everything else in the world with those two things. Why weren't they enough to save Gareth?'

'I don't know,' Rosa said, her voice small.

But Jude knew. He knew exactly why. 'It *was* working. Until I met you. It was like you took over my whole world, in that instant. And I stopped keeping my promise because I needed to be with you.' Rosa started to speak, but he cut across her. 'Oh, I know you weren't there when he died. But I was so caught up in my own misery about you leaving that I *still* didn't see what was right in front of my face.'

Rosa pulled away. 'So, you blame me for Gareth's death?'

Jude looked up at her, beautiful in the moonlight, and knew how unfair he was being. Reaching up, he pulled her back down to him. 'No. No, I don't blame you. I blame myself.' And he always would, whenever he remembered that image of Gareth being wheeled out of the awards ceremony in a body bag.

The next day, the calls had started, asking about what happened next for the band, and the others had nominated him as the new frontman without his even being there.

'I wanted to stop,' he said, softly. 'Afterwards.

I wanted to walk away from it all. The band, music, everything.'

'What changed your mind?' Rosa's voice was still quiet, as if she didn't fully believe him about where the blame lay.

'The rest of the band. They told me…' He swallowed. 'They told me that I had to carry on. For Gareth. To achieve all the dreams he never would, now. It took me a while to believe them. But then one morning, about four months afterwards, I just woke up and knew they were right. Gareth and I had talked about making our band a success our whole lives, it seemed. I couldn't give up on that now. He'd never forgive me. I'd let him down so badly… I had to do anything I could to keep his memory and his dreams alive.'

Rosa's eyes were sad, and she kissed him so sweetly he knew that it had to be pity.

'Gareth loved you,' she said, and he believed her. 'He'd want you to be happy, more than anything else.'

'I know that.'

'Then why are you going back to New York?'

It shouldn't be so hard to think of an answer to that question that she'd accept. 'Because it's my home, now. The band are there. I couldn't leave them—or the music—now. I have an obligation—to them, and to Gareth's memory. And there are the contracts with the label, of course. I owe them all.'

'You sound like Anna,' Rosa said, softly.

Jude shook his head. 'This is different. This is my dream.' His and Gareth's dream. And he would live it for both of them.

'Then why do you look like you've been caged?'

There wasn't an answer at all for that one. 'Go on, then. What do *you* think I should do?'

'I don't know.' Rosa gave a one-shouldered shrug. 'I've spent pretty much my whole adult life avoiding getting trapped that way.'

And she'd keep avoiding it, he knew. Once the wedding was over she'd leave him again.

But this time, he knew that ahead of time. Which meant he wasn't going to waste a moment of the time they had together.

'I don't want to talk about New York any more,' he said. 'Or the past.'

Rosa raised an eyebrow. 'Oh? What do you want to talk about?'

'Honestly?' Jude ran his hands up the side of her naked body. 'I don't want to talk at all.'

'Works for me,' Rosa said, and kissed him.

The bridal party were due to arrive after lunch, so Rosa and Jude spent the following morning putting the finishing touches to the bridal bungalow, and hanging the more delicate decorations for the main function areas that had been left until the last moment, just in case. Basically making sure everything was hashtag perfect for Valentina's arrival.

Anna had already stopped by three times to check on their work, but even that couldn't dim Rosa's mood today. Every action, every moment seemed to remind her of the night before—of being wild and free, first in the sea, and then in Jude's arms. Even the darker turn the conversation had taken…as upsetting as it was to hear about Gareth's death from Jude's own lips, to hear how he blamed himself, she was glad that she knew, now. And if anything, it had only made her feel closer to him again. As if they were finding their way back to how they'd been three years ago, before she walked away.

He said he didn't blame her for distracting him from Gareth's slide into addiction again, and she wanted to believe him. And for now, that would have to be enough. It wasn't as if they had for ever for him to throw blame back at her. They had another week or two at most, and Rosa had very firm ideas about how they should spend that time.

She stretched up to secure a string of tiny lights, and felt a muscle ache, a physical reminder of her actions the night before, and smiled.

'You're doing it again,' Jude said, from across the way.

'Doing what?'

'Distracting me.'

Rosa laughed, just a little uneasily, given her earlier thoughts. 'I can't help that, I'm afraid.'

But Jude grinned back, and she knew he wasn't thinking about Gareth at all. That was good. As much as he'd loved his friend, he couldn't spend the rest of his life in mortgage to his memory.

It all felt so different this time, she realised, for all that it was the same. This time she was older and, yes, maybe even wiser. She didn't have to be afraid of getting drawn in and tied down to Jude. They both knew what this was— an island fling. When it was over they'd go their own ways, still friends, she hoped. It was a better ending than she'd ever hoped for, after she'd left him in London three years before.

And in the meantime…she intended to enjoy every moment they had together. The time limit made everything more intense, in her experience. That was why she kept reliving the night before over and over in her head. Why she couldn't wait for night to fall again so she could take him to bed…

'Right. Is that it?' Jude jumped down from the chair he was standing on and Rosa bit her lip as his loose shirt rode up displaying those tight abs again. Tonight... 'Are we done?' Jude asked, dragging her back to the present.

Rosa checked her clipboard for the list Anna had given her, and scanned the area they'd been working on. 'Believe it or not, I think we are.'

'In that case, I'm off to take a shower.' Jude tossed her a smile as he started unbuttoning his shirt halfway to the path. 'I'd invite you to join me, but there's no way you'd ever be ready to meet the bridal party then.'

'Mmm, probably not,' Rosa agreed, her eyes still fixed on his chest. 'Tonight, though?'

'Definitely tonight,' Jude agreed. 'I'm hoping you might even show me where that secret door that leads to your bedroom is...'

'Ha! You should be so lucky.'

In two swift strides, Jude headed back into the courtyard and kissed her. Thoroughly. 'Oh, I am.'

Rosa smiled after him as he finally left. Then she ran into the villa, through the secret door, and up the twisting wooden stairs to her childhood bedroom in the turret to get ready herself.

'It looks good down here,' Anna said as Rosa appeared. 'And you look nice, too, actually.'

'Thanks,' Rosa said, surprised by the unexpected compliment. She'd dressed in a hot-pink sundress she had a feeling that Jude might enjoy stripping off her later. Her wet hair was piled up in a messy bun, and her make-up was minimal, but she felt beautiful all the same. As if she was glowing.

And she knew that was all down to Jude.

'Their boat arrived a few minutes ago,' Anna said, all business again. 'I've got four staff members down there taking their stuff to the bungalows, and another one bringing them straight here for welcome drinks.' She indicated the table set up with pink champagne in flutes, just inside the courtyard.

Rosa heard a noise further down the path from the villa and stepped forward to the open doorway. 'Here they come.'

'Okay.' Anna took an audible breath.

'Are you *nervous*?' Rosa asked. She wasn't sure she'd ever seen that emotion in her sister before.

'Of course not.'

And then it was too late to press the issue, because the bride—instantly recognised from a million online photos—and her bridesmaids were there, all giggling and talking over each other.

Anna stepped forward and introduced herself to Valentina, who took her hand and pulled her into a hug. 'The island looks so beautiful! Thank you so much for managing to fit us in here for the wedding. It means so much to me and Todd!'

'It's our pleasure,' Anna said, sidestepping the weeks and weeks of work it had taken to be ready for the wedding.

Mind you, given how much Valentina was paying for the privilege, Rosa supposed that was only fair.

'This is my sister, Rosa,' Anna said, and Rosa braced herself for the over-enthusiastic welcome hug from the Internet sensation. 'Now, if you'd like to come through to the courtyard we have welcome drinks for you all, before we take you down to get settled into your accommodation before tonight's dinner.'

'It seems to be going okay,' Rosa murmured to her sister half an hour later, as waiters topped up the glasses of the bridal party—all except Valentina, who was far too busy opening last-minute wedding-week presents from her friends to hold a glass. So far she'd opened mono-grammed slippers, robe, nightdress and under-wear. Rosa was almost afraid to see what was in the last packages.

'It does.' Anna sounded relieved. 'And here come our men,' she added, nodding in the di-rection of the arch from the villa.

Rosa didn't correct her. Just the sight of Jude standing beside Leo on the edge of the courtyard, pale where the other man was tan, but both tall and broad and gorgeous.

Except neither of them were looking at her or Anna.

Leo, understandably, headed straight for his sister, embracing her warmly. Seeing them together actually made Rosa feel a little brighter about the possibilities for her own sister's relationship. Maybe there was more to Leo than the gossip websites would have her believe.

But when she watched Jude, her optimism for their own fling took a little knock.

How had she forgotten, even in her happy haze of lust, that his ex-girlfriend would be here? She scanned the gaggle of bridesmaids and picked out the only redhead. Sylvie Rockwell-Smythe, even more beautiful in real life than she was in her photos.

Why hadn't she prepared herself better for this? Because she didn't want to imagine it, Rosa admitted to herself. And because her time together with Jude here felt like such an escape from the real world, she didn't want any of it to intrude on it.

But when the tall, willowy redhead squealed with delight and ran across to embrace Jude, Rosa was pretty sure reality had come to find them.

'Jude!' Valentina broke off from opening

presents to welcome him, too, the redhead still hanging off his arm. 'Sylvie didn't tell me you were coming! How wonderful!'

'I didn't know!' Sylvie gushed. She batted Jude on the arm. 'He must have flown out here to surprise me.'

Rosa winced, thankful that Anna had headed inside to deal with the catering staff and wasn't there to see this.

'Not exactly,' Jude said, his voice cool.

'Sorry?' Sylvie's brows knitted together without wrinkling her forehead at all.

Suddenly Rosa looked up to find Jude's gaze on her, his eyes beckoning her over as he disentangled himself from Sylvie's hands. 'Sylvie, Valentina, have you met Rosa Gray?'

CHAPTER NINE

THE FIRST THING that struck Jude as he reached the courtyard was the noise—the high, excited voices of Valentina and her bridesmaids, so different from Rosa's warm, low, laughing tones. And then he saw her—Sylvie—her bright red hair and perfect body shining in the Spanish sunlight.

He'd thought he might love her, once, he remembered, but somehow it no longer felt real. Nothing from that world did—not when compared to swimming naked in the ocean with Rosa, with holding Rosa in his arms.

That was real. *Rosa* was real.

But it was Sylvie throwing herself into his arms, believing he'd arrived on the island just to surprise her.

Well, that was a misunderstanding he could clear up right away.

'Sylvie, Valentina, have you met Rosa Gray?' He gazed at Rosa, loving how she knew what he wanted, was almost halfway across the court-yard before he said her name.

He just hoped she'd play along a little longer.

'We have,' Valentina said, smiling happily, as a bride-to-be should. 'So, is she what brought you to this beautiful island—if you're not here for my wedding?'

'Jude and I are old friends,' Rosa said, return-ing an equally warm smile as she took his arm, pressing close in a way that showed everyone exactly what sort of *friends* they were. Jude's heart seemed to settle back into a rhythm he hadn't known it had lost as she touched him.

'I thought I'd come spend a few weeks here visiting with Rosa this summer,' Jude said, lightly. 'It seemed like a good time to be out of New York.'

Sylvie's cheeks flushed a little at that, and Valentina gave them both a knowing look.

'I heard about the book,' she said. 'I didn't read it, of course. But it does seem to be every-where at the moment.'

Strange to think that Valentina had built an entire career out of letting people see into her life—every moment, photographed and filtered and shared.

'How do you cope with it?' he asked, sud-denly. 'Everyone knowing every single thing that happens in your life, I mean?'

Valentina laughed. 'Oh, Jude. They know what I *want* them to know. That's the joy of controlling your own brand, the way I do. They never see more than I'm willing to show them.'

'You show them a lot, though,' Rosa pointed out.

Valentina shrugged her slim shoulders. 'I owe them a lot. It's only fair that I share plenty in return. But that doesn't mean I don't get to keep a few of my own secrets.'

Jude was glad, he realised. He'd hate for Valentina to feel the way he did—as if every inch of his personal space had been invaded, every precious memory passed from person to person to examine.

Rosa squeezed his arm, and he found himself grateful again that the author of *The Naked Truth* had never found out about her. Maybe he still had a few secrets left, too.

'Now, I hope you'll join us for the wedding anyway, since you're here?' Valentina asked.

'I'd hate to intrude,' Jude started, but Valentina laughed.

'Don't be silly! The more the merrier. And of course, if you'd like to bring a plus-one, I'm sure that would be fine…'

'Then thank you,' Jude said, already calculating in his mind how happy Robyn would be about this one.

Being seen at the wedding of the year could never be a bad thing. And having a beautiful woman like Rosa on his arm had to look good, too.

The fact it would rub Sylvie's nose in it a bit felt pretty great, too, if he was brutally honest.

Leaving Valentina and her bridesmaids to the presents, Jude led Rosa off to the shadows of the villa.

'So, that's the ex, huh?' she asked, glancing back out at them. 'She's beautiful. Like, absurdly so. Even more than the photos.'

'She's nothing compared to you,' Jude said, making her laugh, although he couldn't figure out why.

'She's a model, Jude. A six-foot-tall, beautiful, willowy redhead with perfect hair and a dozen modelling contracts. I am under no illusions about my own charms, but they're not a patch on hers. You don't need to lie to me to make me feel good.'

'I'm not lying,' Jude said, holding her close so she had to look into his eyes and see the truth of it. 'Yes, Sylvie looks beautiful. She's stunning.'

'Not helping with the not lying part.'

'But you...' He stared down into her wide, dark eyes, her long lashes sooty against her skin, trying to find the words. 'You're *alive*. You have so much life, so much vibrancy... She could never match that. She *looks* beautiful. You live it.'

He must have said something right, from the way she kissed him.

'You're such a *poet*,' she said, fondly.

'So you'll come to the wedding with me? It won't be any fun without you.'

Rosa pulled a face. 'I'll need to check with Anna. I'm supposed to be working that day, of course.'

'But she'll be going with Leo, surely?'

'That's true. I'll ask her, I promise.'

'Tonight?'

The smile Rosa gave him reminded him they had other plans for tonight. 'Maybe tomorrow.'

'Tomorrow works for me.'

'Anna, have you got a minute?' Rosa had been looking all over the island for her sister after another day of work. Anna had been strangely absent for most of it, until Rosa finally spotted her heading down the path to the jetty.

'Not now.' Anna didn't even look back at her. Wasn't that always the way with her? She wanted to organise her life for her, but only when it suited her.

Rosa took a breath and reminded herself she was asking Anna for a favour. She needed to keep her cool. 'It's about Jude. Valentina has asked him to the wedding and he wants me to be his plus-one. Will that be a problem? I can still oversee the seating charts and things, and you'll be there with Leo anyway…'

Anna finally glanced back, pushing her hair out of her eyes. 'Leo hasn't mentioned me accompanying him to the wedding,' she said slowly. 'We're not, I mean, it's not serious.'

If Leo and Anna weren't serious, then what on earth did that make her and Jude? 'Oh, come on, I've seen the way he looks at you.'

'It's not serious,' Anna repeated, and Rosa decided to worry later about whatever games her sister was playing now.

'If you say so. So you don't mind? It turns out Jude knows Valentina quite well, he used to go out with one of the bridesmaids—the redhead who complained that the bed is too hard and that we haven't provided the right range of herbal teas—and it ended, well, horrifically. Long story short, she was involved with the book, so it's a pride thing to accept the invite and bring a date, I guess. But what with the way we left things, I think…'

Anna held up her hand to silence her, and Rosa got the feeling she was mentally counting to ten, as she used to when they were small. 'Rosa, fill me in later. I have to go over to the mainland and I hate sailing over in the dark. Yes, go to the wedding. It's fine.'

The mainland? What on earth could she be going there for? Everything for the wedding had already been delivered. Unless this wasn't to do with the wedding...

'What's so urgent?' Rosa's voice sharpened, as she took in her sister's appearance for the first time. 'Are you okay? You're very pale. Do you feel ill?'

'Rosa, don't fuss. I just have to do something.' Yeah, that wasn't very reassuring—especially if Anna didn't want to tell her what she needed to do.

'I really think you should wait till morning.' Then, as Anna shook her head, 'In that case I'm coming with you. I'll drive the boat. The way you look you won't be able to get it out of the harbour!'

Anna wanted to refuse, Rosa could tell. But she wasn't going to let her.

Not waiting for an answer, Rosa took the boat key out of Anna's hand and led her the rest of the way down to the jetty. It was pretty clear that Anna didn't want to talk about whatever was going on, so Rosa didn't press her for details, concentrating instead on steering the dinghy over the short distance as speedily as possible. She pulled up alongside the jetty on the mainland with a smooth flourish. 'Right, where next? Anna, I'm coming with you. Don't argue.'

Anna opened her mouth to protest and then shut it again. Rosa smiled. For once, she was in charge.

Sancia always kept a car in the car park near the jetty, for whenever they needed to run errands on the mainland, and Rosa was relieved to see it there waiting for them. Anna pulled the key to Sancia's ancient rusty small car from her pocket and handed it to her, not responding as Rosa's hand closed over hers with what she hoped was a reassuring squeeze.

'The town,' she said, her voice husky. 'The pharmacy. There's one on the retail park this side of town, it's not far.'

The pharmacy. Oh, that didn't sound good at all.

Now Rosa was really worried.

The roads were deserted and it didn't take long to clear the small village and head towards the town. Rosa drove at her normal speed—ten kilometres above the speed limit—more concerned by the fact that Anna wasn't issuing her usual warnings to drive carefully than by the sharp turns and corners.

Something was definitely wrong here.

Spotting the retail park, and the pharmacy,

Rosa swung the car into a free space and killed the engine. 'Do you want me to come in with you?'

'No. Thanks.' Anna made no move to get out of the car, though.

'Anna, let me go.' Rosa had a feeling she knew exactly what this was. And it was bigger than any argument that had ever been between them. 'Do you need me to buy you a pregnancy test? Is that what's happening here?' What else could it be? Rosa knew that panicked, lost look on her sister's face. She'd seen it on her own, once.

Anna froze. 'Leo doesn't want a family.' Rosa had a feeling that wasn't what Anna had intended to say. 'He'll think I've betrayed him.'

'Anna, honey, it takes two to make a baby. Leo's a grown man. If you are pregnant, he'll understand.' And if he didn't, then Rosa would beat understanding into him. Not that she was going to mention that part to Anna yet.

'No, he won't. He told me from the start, no promises, no commitment. It's bad enough I've fallen in love with him. How can I be so stupid as to get pregnant, too? It's like Sebastian all over again, only much, much worse. I only *thought* I loved Sebastian.'

Okay, *that* was a surprise. But actually, it explained a lot. 'You were pregnant back then?

Why didn't you tell me? Why do you never let anyone help, Anna?' The old frustrations rose up in her. If she'd known, she could have helped. She could have done *something*. 'You don't have to do it all alone. You don't have to be perfect. You can ask for help…'

'Last time I needed your help you walked away.' It was always going to come down to that between them, wasn't it?

Rosa bit her lip. Anna was never going to understand why she couldn't stay. And now really wasn't the time to confess all the other reasons—the ones that had nothing to do with Anna or their father. 'Things were complicated then. I'm sorry. But I'm here now and, I promise you, you're not alone. Now let me go and get the test for you and then, if you are, we'll figure out what to do. And if you're not then you and I need to have a long-overdue talk. Deal?'

'Deal.' Anna squeezed her hand tightly.

Rosa got out of the car and jogged over to the pharmacy. She might have let her sister down before, but Anna wouldn't have to worry about that this time.

And nor would her child, with Rosa as their auntie.

Something was up with Rosa.

Jude surveyed her over the rack of Scrabble

tiles, ignoring the letters and potential words to consider the woman sitting across from him instead. On either side of him, Sancia and Ernest Gray were debating whether whatever obscure word the professor had come up with existed in the *Oxford English Dictionary*. Jude was fairly sure it didn't—the professor was a terrible Scrabble cheat.

The bigger mystery to him was what Rosa was thinking about.

Whatever it was, it had distracted her completely, all evening. She'd barely responded to his hand on her hip as they walked to the table, she'd had nothing to say over dinner, and now she'd barely managed more than a three-letter word all game.

Scrabble, Jude had discovered to his surprise, was the one area of the world where Professor Gray and his youngest daughter actually seemed to connect. He and Sancia usually just muddled through trying to keep up. They both fought for every tile, every triple word score, every definition.

But not tonight.

Suddenly Rosa looked up, her attention drawn by something by the darkened arch leading out of the courtyard. Jude twisted in his seat to try and see what had distracted her.

Anna. Of course. And Leo, leading her away.

Jude turned back to Rosa to see an unfamiliar look on her face. Part hope, part fear, and all uncertainty.

'I'm going to go and fetch my dictionary,' Sancia said, rising from her seat. The professor followed her, arguing that since it probably wasn't the *Oxford English Dictionary* it wouldn't count, anyway.

Jude waited until the others were safely inside the villa before he slid over to Sancia's chair and reached for Rosa's hand.

'What's up?'

'Hmm?' Rosa turned to him, blinking. 'Nothing.'

'Liar.' She'd never lied to him before, that he knew of. Let him believe things that wouldn't happen, sure, but that was his false hope, not her fault. Now he was really worried.

But Rosa looked down at the table and said, 'Sorry. You're right. It's just… I'm not sure it's my secret to tell.'

Something relaxed inside him. That he, of all people, could understand. 'That's fine. But if it'll help to talk about it…you know I'm not one to share other people's stories.'

'I do know.' Rosa gave him a warm smile, then glanced back towards the villa. 'Come on, let's go. Take a walk or something.'

'You always talk better when we're walking.'

Rosa shrugged, getting to her feet. 'You know me. I work better in action.'

'I do,' Jude said, and realised it was true.

He *knew* Rosa, in a way he wasn't sure he'd ever known anyone else. He'd thought it was just because she lived life out loud, her every action proclaiming exactly who she was. But others— her own family—still didn't seem to understand her, even with a lifetime of observing her.

So maybe it was just something about their connection.

Maybe it was just him, and just her.

She led him along the winding path that trailed around the island, through lush foliage and flowers, past the bright white bungalows and their freshly painted shutters, skirting the beaches and waterfronts. When they came too close to the bridal bungalow, Rosa tugged his hand to take a different trail, one that led them away from the laughter and the chatter.

Rosa still wasn't talking, Jude realised. The romantic walk in the moonlight was nice and all, but it wasn't getting him any closer to figuring out what was on Rosa's mind.

'Is it Sylvie?' he asked, figuring he had to start somewhere. 'Has she said anything?'

'Who?' Rosa looked up, surprised. 'Oh, no. Not her.'

Of course. Because that would mean her actually being affected by his ex-girlfriend being on the island, and they'd both been very clear that this wasn't that kind of relationship.

Then he remembered the way she'd watched Anna and Leo leaving the courtyard. 'Your sister, then?'

Rosa didn't answer that time, which was how Jude knew he'd got it right.

'What did she do?' He could feel his irritation with Rosa's sister rising. Whatever their differences, Rosa had busted a gut helping her get the island ready for the wedding, and Anna had still managed to find fault at every turn.

'She got pregnant,' Rosa said, her voice soft, and all of Jude's anger faded away in an instant.

'Are you sure?'

Rosa shook her head. 'I took her to buy the test last night. She didn't tell me the outcome but…you saw her with Leo this evening. I could tell from her face, she was going to tell him. So I guess it must have been positive.'

'Wow.' Suddenly, a terrible thought occurred to him, and he tugged her to face him. 'Wait, do we need to—?'

Rosa interrupted him with a shake of her head. 'It's fine.'

'No, but I mean, I know we've been careful since, but that first time. In the sea…'

'Jude. It's covered. Trust me. With travel-

SOPHIE PEMBROKE 175

ling the world and all the different time zones, my body got so confused the doctor put me on a contraceptive injection anyway. There's no chance, this time.'

'Right. Okay, then.' Jude was almost certain that the feeling coursing through him was relief. Just relief. Because disappointment would have been crazy.

If Rosa got pregnant, would she stay? Or, more importantly, would she ever forgive him?

He couldn't think about those impossibilities now.

'How do you think Leo will react?' he asked, instead.

'Anna seemed pretty sure the answer to that is "badly".' She sighed, dropping down to sit on one of the brightly painted benches that studded the island path at points where the view was even more spectacular than the average La Isla Marina vista. 'But he's an idiot if he doesn't just marry her and live happily ever after.'

'I never thought I'd hear you advocating settling down and living the traditional life,' Jude observed. He sat beside her, and she took his hand in hers, absently playing with his fingers.

'Well, not for me,' Rosa admitted. 'But you've seen the two of them together. How they look at each other. To start, I thought Leo was just playing her, but now… I think he genuinely loves her. I just hope he realises that, too.'

'So do I,' Jude said, although he wasn't fully thinking of Anna and Leo.

He was thinking about Rosa. How fiercely he'd fallen for her, three years ago. How the love that had turned to shock and anger had become an aching loss, until he found her again. How, even now, even when he was protecting his heart the best he knew how, he knew it was going to hurt, when she left again.

This time, he realised, he would have to leave first. *He* needed to make that decision, take that control. It was the only way he'd ever be able to live with it.

'I have to admit, though,' Rosa said, staring out at the calm sea before them, 'I am kind of looking forward to being an auntie.'

'You'll be the cool auntie who sends them awesome gifts from all over the world, from places they couldn't even imagine from their boring house in Oxford.'

'Exactly!' Rosa flashed him a grin. 'And maybe…maybe they'll come here on holiday, and I can join them. Like we used to when we were kids.'

'You think you'll come back to the island more often, now?' Jude asked, surprised.

'Maybe.' Because there was never any certainty with Rosa, was there? 'I mean, it's the only place that's ever really felt like home.'

And suddenly, sitting in the moonlight, talking about someone else's child, Jude realised he knew exactly how she felt.

Only, for him, home wasn't a place.

It was a person.

CHAPTER TEN

ALMOST THERE.

Just over twenty-four hours now until the wedding, and Rosa had ticked off the last of the day's jobs on her accursed clipboard. The groom and his family had arrived, and the Spanish-style lunch they'd arranged for the whole wedding party had been a huge success. Four courses over several hours followed by much-needed siestas had made the perfect introduction to the island, and Anna and Rosa had planned for beach games and a much more informal supper to be served at the beach later that evening. The informal evening would not only be fun, but crucially it gave the island staff plenty of time to prepare for the next day, when another hundred guests were due to arrive, and for the wedding ceremony itself, which would begin at seven o'clock tomorrow night.

Rosa had to admit, Anna had pulled off a near miracle. The island looked perfect. Every bungalow was ready and—thanks to her and Jude—every tree had fairy lights threaded through it, and the pagoda and central area were set up for the ceremony and party. Anna had confirmed that Valentina's dress had arrived that day, escorted by a dressmaker who would stay until Valentina was dressed, and last time Rosa had checked in on the kitchens Sancia had been harassing the chefs from Barcelona who were setting up. Fortunately her mother was easily distracted, and the chefs seemed to be working remarkably amicably with the island's own cooks.

Valentina glowed with happiness, her groom's wealthy parents were happy, and the brides-maids—except for Sylvie—full of nothing but praise.

In summary, they were ready. Which meant Rosa was officially free to pursue her own inter-ests for the rest of the evening—namely, Jude.

At least, she was once she'd reported in to her lord and master, Anna.

Rosa smiled to herself as she made her way up the path to the main villa. Actually, things between her and her sister were better than they had been in years—since before their mother left, even. Rosa had managed to get Anna alone the day before and get the full story from her. Yes, she was pregnant. No, she wasn't marry-

ing Leo and living happily ever after. But she
seemed content, all the same. As if the life
within her had settled her—given her a focus
that mattered to *her*, rather than keeping other
people satisfied, as she seemed to with her
work, or looking after their father.

Part of Rosa worried that Anna was just getting tied down in a new way, but the more rea-
sonable part of her knew that this was different.
A *baby* was different, especially for Anna.

But she couldn't stop remembering those terrifying weeks when she'd believed she might
be pregnant with Jude's child. Then, at twenty-
three, it had felt like the end of the world—a
shackle on her life before she'd even figured out
how she wanted to live it.

Now, three years and an awful lot of experience on, she wondered if it might feel different.

Not that she intended to find out. She had
plans, still. Life still to live, adventures still to
have.

When she'd left him, and La Isla Marina, and
everything else behind last time it had been to
find *her* life. The one no one else in the world
could live but her. The person she was meant to
be, even. And, over the last three years, she'd
found it. She had a career she loved, that fulfilled
her—and allowed her to keep moving, to experience new places and cultures and lives. She met

more people from more different walks of life in a month than many people met in their whole existence. She never had to slow down to wait for someone else to catch up, never had to modulate her expectations or her impulses to satisfy someone else. She could be exactly who she was, without judgement. Or at least, without hanging around long enough to hear or care about any judgement anyone passed on her choices.

She had exactly what she'd wanted. Yes, it could be lonely, occasionally. But the benefits outweighed the negatives, right? And if, sometimes, she wondered if it was enough, well, as long as she kept moving she could push those thoughts aside. She didn't want what Anna seemed to—to settle down in one place and live one life with one man. And even then, Leo didn't seem as if he was going to give Anna her happy ever after. If St Anna couldn't make love work, what hope was there for her screw-up little sister?

And besides, even if Rosa and Jude had that sort of relationship—the for ever kind—she couldn't live his life. She couldn't smile politely at self-important celebrities and people trying to tell her what to do. She wasn't that person.

Jude, surprisingly, seemed to be. She'd thought he'd be raging against the requirements and constraints, but it seemed that he liked the fame more than he liked the freedom. Or maybe he just stuck with it for the sake of Gareth's memory. Out of guilt for the promise he broke.

Whatever his reasons, Rosa was never going to be that way. She couldn't be that woman he needed by his side, always.

Even if she wanted to be.

The villa was lit up with tiny lanterns, bright spots in the darkness illuminating the happiness and love that filled the island for Valentina's wedding. Rosa wished some of it could spread to Anna and Leo, but she knew that if it didn't, Anna would be okay. She was strong, and she could organise her way out of any situation.

Anna would be fine.

Rosa stepped through into the courtyard, and saw her sister bending to kiss her parents, one at a time. Which was unusual on many levels. Firstly, Anna wasn't a usually demonstrative person that way, and Rosa knew she didn't intend to tell their parents about the pregnancy until after the wedding, so it couldn't be that. Add in the ongoing weirdness of their estranged parents apparently spending all their time together again, after ten years apart, and Rosa was just baffled. What had happened to her dysfunctional, tension-inducing family? At least she knew what to expect from them. The new dynamics just confused her. Where was she supposed to fit in? Or maybe she wasn't. After all, she'd be gone again soon, and they could all carry on without her, in Oxford and Spain. Rosa knew when she wasn't needed.

She raised an eyebrow at Anna. 'It all looks very cosy in here—everything all right?'

'Everything's good,' Anna said. 'I was just discussing the possibility of staying on the island. After all, it's never been one person's job to run it before.'

Rosa's eyes widened, a hundred questions jostling for attention in her mind while she tried—and failed—to choose one. 'But… Oxford…? Book…? Dad…? Here?'

'Quite,' Anna said enigmatically. 'Did you put the volleyball net up, Rosa? Don't worry, I'll go. I could do with some fresh air.'

And then she was gone, before Rosa could confirm that, yes, actually, she had put the net up. And also, what the hell?

Anna, staying on La Isla Marina, with their mother—and possibly their father, given how things were going—and her baby.

Anna, who for the last decade had focussed on exactly the same sort of academic success that had driven their father for so long—and driven their parents apart.

Maybe this was proof that people could

change, after all. And for some reason, it made Rosa incredibly uncomfortable.

If Anna could change, did that mean *she* could? More to the point, that she *should*?

No. Rosa had fought too hard to be exactly who she was to give it up now.

'I'm going to go and help her,' Rosa said, but her parents weren't even listening. They were lost in their own conversation.

Rosa walked back out onto the island proper and sucked in a deep breath. Anna didn't need her help, because there was nothing to help with. Everything was done and ready, and the staff they had in place would be running the events perfectly. If Anna was there, she didn't need Rosa's help.

So she turned away from the public areas and all the fun wedding events, and headed down the path towards Jude's bungalow by the sea, hoping she could lose herself in his arms for a while, and forget all the questions buzzing in her head.

Jude was sitting at the patio table when she arrived, his guitar resting on his knee as he noted something down in the brown leather notebook on the table.

Rosa leant against the wall of the bungalow and watched him as he picked out a melody on the strings, before stopping to write down something else. He was so handsome. Beautiful, even, in a way she'd never imagined a man could be. If she had her camera with her, she'd frame him against the night sky, the fairy lights behind him, highlighting the planes and shadows of that beautiful face.

It seemed strange now, to remember that he hadn't always been the star. The frontman of The Swifts, taking all the praise and glory. When he'd been in Gareth's shadow, others had barely even seemed to notice him.

But to Rosa, Jude had always been that bright, shining star in the darkness.

'Working?' she asked, softly, so as not to startle him.

Jude looked up and smiled. 'Playing, really.'

He strummed the melody again, carrying on for longer this time, the music almost familiar somehow.

'Do I know that one?' she asked, slipping into the seat opposite him.

'Parts of it, probably,' Jude admitted. 'It's a variation on a theme—I'm playing around with some of the local music here.'

'For the new album?'

Jude shook his head, looking down at the strings so his dark hair fell across his forehead. 'Just for me, really. I doubt the rest of the band would think this fitted with our brand.'

'Brand?' Rosa pulled a face. It always came back to that for him, it seemed. Trying to fit into a mould that he'd outgrown, even if he didn't realise it. 'Can't you just play the music you like?'

'Apparently not. At least, not back in New York. Here, however...' He strummed the strings again, making Rosa smile.

'Play me a song. One just for me.'

'Sure.' As he started to play Rosa stood up and made her way through the open patio doors into the bungalow bedroom, stripping her dress from her body as she went. The music stuttered for a second, then continued, Jude lifting his voice to join it, singing of beauty and life and water and sun.

Naked, Rosa stretched out on Jude's bed and gazed back at him, watching as he created something entirely new, something just for her. After a few lines, he looked up and met her gaze, and suddenly it wasn't her lack of clothes that made her feel exposed.

It was his eyes. The way he looked deep into the heart of her, the way no one else ever managed. She kept moving, kept talking, kept living, and no one ever kept up with her well enough to see the truth in her. But with Jude, she was frozen. Motionless. Naked—physically and emotionally.

He saw everything. And he sang it back to her.

Rosa wasn't sure if that was terrifying or wonderful.

Maybe it was both.

The song came to an end, but Jude's gaze didn't leave hers. 'That what you wanted?'

'Yes,' she said, even though she wasn't sure she should have asked for it. 'At least, the first part of what I wanted.'

'Oh? What's the second part?' Jude asked, but she could tell from his smile that he already knew.

Still, she opened her arms to him to make it clear. 'You. Here. Now.'

Jude put his guitar back in its case, closing it hurriedly. 'I can do that.'

'You know, we're really, really good at that,' Jude said, running his hands over the smooth expanses of Rosa's skin, just because he could. For now, she was all his, here in his bed, in his arms. Like a song he never wanted to end.

'We really are.' Rosa twisted in his arms so she faced him, pressing a kiss against his chest.

He wanted to say it. Wanted to tell her that it didn't have to end, that she didn't have to run. That they could try a life together, for real, this time.

But he'd already said it all in his song. He'd

poured his every emotion, every thought into that melody and those lyrics, sung his heart to her. She knew it all already. And if it didn't change her mind, he still needed to be able to walk away with his heart intact.

So he said nothing.

'Anna's decided to stay on the island,' Rosa said, suddenly, bringing Jude back to the here and now.

'Really? Because of the baby?'

'I guess.'

'You sound confused.' Was it just the idea of voluntarily staying on one sleepy island for ever that confused her? Or was there something more to this?

'No... I get it. I think.' Rosa sighed, and pulled away, sitting up and tugging the sheet up over her body, which Jude thought was a crying shame. 'No, I don't. As long as I can remember, Anna wanted to be an academic like Dad, living in Oxford, researching, writing her books and teaching her students. And now... she's changing her whole life.'

'Love makes us do strange things.' Jude's throat felt tight as he said it.

Rosa gave him a strange look. 'Leo's not staying with her.'

'I meant the love of her baby,' Jude explained. 'Although...she's heartbroken, remember. She probably imagined a whole future with Leo and now she's reassessing. She's finding a new future for a new her.'

'You sound like you know what she's going through,' Rosa said, curiously. 'Who did you love?'

'You.' He'd said it before he even realised he was going to. The horror in Rosa's eyes made it clear he had to take it back, though. And fast. 'Once, anyway. I mean, when you left last time. But that was a long time ago now.' He kept his voice as casual as he could, a careful eye on Rosa's face to watch the shock and fear subsiding.

'Yes. A long time ago.' Something flashed across her face though, something deeper than the horror.

'What?' Sitting up, he pulled her close again, needing her touch. 'What is it?'

'When I left… I did it badly, I know that.'

'It was a long time ago, Rosa. It doesn't matter now.' Even if she'd stayed, what would it have changed, really? Gareth would still have died, that much he realised now, seeing her again. She'd given him some peace with that, at least. But if she'd come back, how long would it have lasted? Another month? A year, if he was lucky? The axe would have fallen sooner or later, and later would have only hurt more.

'But that's the thing—it does.' She looked up into his eyes. 'I need to explain.'

'You already have,' Jude pointed out. 'You told me exactly why you left.' And to be honest, he wasn't sure he could hear it again—listen to her say how little he'd meant to her that she moved on without a backward glance, just because she didn't like to stay in one place too long.

'I didn't tell you everything.'

Her quiet words stopped his brain in its tracks. Leaning back against the pillows, he pulled her down with him, holding her tight against his shoulder. 'Tell me now?' He wasn't sure he wanted to hear it, but he knew he needed to know it.

Rosa nodded, her hair brushing his skin. And Jude waited to hear the truth.

'When I left, for my *abuelo*'s funeral… I planned to come back. I was going to come back to you.'

It was as if the world starting falling into place. As a discordant tune became a melody as the right notes were played instead.

He'd known it wasn't right. Known there was something wrong about her leaving like that. Their connection had been too strong for her to sever it so thoughtlessly.

Yes, he'd known that Rosa wouldn't stay for

ever. She wasn't the sort of woman to settle down, and he'd accepted that. But he'd expected more from her than for her to just drop out of his life—that was the part that had haunted him for the past three years.

And now, it seemed, he was about to learn the truth about why.

'Why didn't you?' he asked, dreading and needing the answer in equal measure.

'Because I was scared,' Rosa admitted. 'What I felt for you…it was all-encompassing, and it scared me. When I was with you, I couldn't think about anything else. Couldn't remember who I was, what *I* wanted out of life. I was afraid that if I came back to you I wouldn't be able to leave again, and I knew I needed to, if I wanted to follow my dreams. And then—' She broke off.

'What?' He needed it all. Every detail. Even as his body buzzed with the knowledge that it wasn't just him. She'd felt it, too.

Whether she admitted it or not, Rosa had loved him, too. And it still hadn't been enough for her to stay.

'I was late. My body…all the stress of the funeral, and the fight with Anna, I guess it got to it. I was two weeks late and I thought…'

'You thought you were pregnant.' For a moment, the image of a tiny little girl with Rosa's dark eyes and hair flashed through his head. *There's no chance, this time*. That was what she'd said, when he'd asked if they needed to be concerned. And this was what she'd meant.

How could he not have seen that?

'I wasn't,' Rosa said, quickly dispelling the image. 'But the thought that I could have been... I realised how careless we'd been. How when I was with you I set aside everything I wanted for myself, every dream I had, every promise I'd made to myself that I wouldn't get tied down to a life of someone else's choosing, like Mama and Anna did. I forgot everything that made me Rosa, and that terrified me. So I ran.'

The worst part was, it all made perfect sense, in a Rosa sort of way. Of course she had run.

'I wish you'd been able to tell me, back then.' Jude's head was still spinning, imagining a world in which she might have done.

How could things have been different? Was there any way this could have ended differently?

Knowing Rosa, and knowing himself, he suspected not.

He'd been chasing fame, and she'd been chasing freedom. They couldn't have done that together, not really. He could never have asked Rosa to chase his dreams with him instead of hers, and she could never have asked him to abandon his, either. Especially not after Gareth died, and he had two people's dreams to chase already.

The worst part was, nothing had changed. They were the same people they'd been three years ago.

There was still only one way this could all end.

'I wish I had, too,' Rosa said. 'I know it wouldn't have changed anything, but still… I wish I hadn't left things the way I did.'

Jude rolled over so she was lying underneath him. 'I think we've more than made up for it, the last couple of weeks. Don't you think?'

'Definitely.' Rosa smiled up at him, so sweetly that he had to kiss her. 'But we could probably stand to make up a few more times, before we leave. Don't you think?'

That, Jude decided, was a question better answered with action, than words.

CHAPTER ELEVEN

THE WEDDING WAS PERFECT.

The sun shone down on the evening service, while Valentina and Todd took their vows with laughter and joy in between the serious moments. The actual, legal part of the ceremony, Rosa knew, had been completed in New York a week or so ago. So technically, Valentina and Todd were already tied to each other for life. But today was the day that mattered most to them—the day where they confirmed that commitment to everyone who mattered to them. When they stood proud and said, 'I've made my decision. It's this person for me. For ever.'

Rosa tried to imagine being that sure of anything, but the only thing that came to mind was Jude. And they both already knew that wasn't an option. So instead, she decided to just enjoy the day.

Valentina looked more beautiful than ever, Rosa thought, in her designer dress. The white bodice clung to her curves before flaring out into a full, knee-length skirt. But it was the sheer overdress with its embroidered flowers, bold and beautiful in a red that matched the bridesmaids' dresses, that really made it something special.

Rosa took a perverse pleasure in the fact that Sylvie's dress clashed horribly with her hair.

Her own lemon-yellow sundress was maybe a little casual for such a celebrity wedding, but she hadn't exactly packed for the occasion. She'd made an extra effort with her hair, though, braiding it carefully and threading tiny white flowers through it. If she was here as Jude's date, even just for the day, she wanted to look as if she belonged with him.

And Jude was, quite frankly, breathtaking. While the groom's party were all in pale linen suits, Jude wore a darker charcoal suit in the same light material. His white shirt was open at the collar and his skin, while darkened a little by his time on the island, was still pale enough to make his blue eyes blaze against it, and the darkness of his hair.

It was strange, being at the wedding as a guest instead of an employee of the island. Stranger still to see Anna in her uniform of dark skirt and white blouse, her dark hair pulled severely back. Rosa kept wanting to go and help—to fetch more ice, or fix a torn hem, or mop up a spill. But instead, her job for the day was to hang off Jude's arm, look pretty and annoy his ex.

She could do that. For one day, anyway. For one day, it was a novelty. Any more, though, and she knew she'd be bored rigid.

As the sky darkened, the party went on. Food was served, music was played, speeches made. Valentina and Todd had already performed their first dance—a very location-appropriate tango, with enough heat in it that Rosa had caught Jude's eye and made a mental promise for later.

'Jude!' Valentina approached them, her hand still tightly clutching Todd's. She was beaming, happiness glowing from every inch of her. 'Isn't everything going wonderfully?'

'It's been a beautiful day,' Jude agreed, his hand resting on Rosa's thigh.

'And it's not over yet! Speaking of which… Since you're here, do you think you might be able to treat us to a song or two? Since it *is* my wedding day…'

Jude laughed. 'How can I refuse a request from the bride? Especially since I gatecrashed your wedding in the first place.' He smiled at Rosa. 'As long as you're okay here alone?'

'Absolutely.' Rosa relaxed further back into

her chair. 'I'm going to sit here and keep eating these dessert canapés. You can come roll me into bed when you're done.'

'It's a deal.' Jude pressed a kiss to her lips, and disappeared off to fetch his guitar.

'You realise that when he goes back to New York he'll forget all about you.' Rosa's spine stiffened as Sylvie slipped into Jude's abandoned chair. 'When he's deep in his music he forgets almost everything.'

Rosa shrugged. 'That's not a problem for us.'

'Because you're *so* different?' Sylvie's laughter was sharp and ugly. 'Trust me, every woman thinks that.'

'No,' Rosa said, patiently. 'Because when he goes back to New York I'll be heading off somewhere else, on my next assignment. Russia, I think, this time.'

That, at least, seemed to surprise her. 'You're not planning on coming to New York with him if he asks?'

'He won't ask,' Rosa said, with certainty. 'Mostly because he knows I won't go. I have my life and he has his. It just so happens that they both intersected here for a while. That's all.'

'Do you honestly believe that you'll walk away from here and forget all about him?'

'Maybe not forget,' Rosa admitted. After all, she'd never forgotten him in the three years they were apart. There was no reason to imagine she would this time. 'But I have plenty of other things in my life to focus on. I can't see me having time to pine, if that's what you're worried about.'

Except for all those nights, alone in a hotel room or a tent, remembering. Those were always the hardest.

'Worried? No.' Sylvie gave her a shark-bright smile. 'Relieved. If you're out of the picture in New York that gives me an opening.'

'Even if he forgets you for his music?' Rosa ignored the burning feeling in her chest that started when she imagined Jude and Sylvie together in New York. He wouldn't go back to her, would he? Not after everything she'd done. 'Do you think he'll even want to see you, after all the stories you sold about him?'

Sylvie dismissed both concerns with a wave of her hand. 'Honestly, it's more about the picture than the truth. As long as he's seen with me enough to get our photo everywhere it's good for both of us. The rest is almost beside the point.'

Beside the point. All the wonderful things she'd shared with Jude were, to Sylvie, unimportant beside his fame.

How could she ever explain to someone like that how Jude's fame was the least attractive thing about him, to her? Because it was his celebrity, his success, that meant he was tied to a life that would mean she would always have to follow. To be Jude Alexander's partner, instead of her own person.

And she couldn't do that.

A cheer went up around the crowd as Jude stepped onto the small makeshift stage the traditional Spanish band had used earlier. Sylvie disappeared, off into the crowd, presumably to be seen with someone more deserving. And Rosa settled back down to listen to Jude play.

He started with a familiar song—one of The Swifts' most classic numbers, but played in an acoustic style that rendered it almost something different altogether. Rosa had listened to plenty of Jude's band's music—it was hard to avoid anywhere where music was played, like hotel bars and supermarkets, not to mention the car radio. Sometimes, when she really wanted to torture herself, she'd even look him up online and read interviews with him, looking for the man she'd once known. The photos she'd taken on tour with them, what seemed like a lifetime ago now, showed a different man altogether, she always thought. Before fame hit, and the Jude the public saw became more polished, more careful.

But she'd never heard the songs this way

before—just Jude and his guitar. There was so much more emotion in the music, she thought. They felt raw, but real, without all the production and effects added to the finished pieces.

She preferred them this way, she decided. But maybe that wasn't surprising. She preferred the man playing them to the one Sylvie described as Jude in New York.

The next song he played, though, sounded different again. Mostly because the last time she'd heard it, Gareth had been the one singing it. Rosa caught Jude's eye and saw all the emotions there. Had he ever even played this song since Gareth's death? Probably not, knowing Jude.

But maybe it was time. He'd said he wanted to find closure on the island, to face his demons. Coming to terms with what had happened to Gareth had to be a big part of that.

Rosa hoped it was helping. She wanted Jude happy, even if she wouldn't be there to see it.

Suddenly, Leo pulled a chair up next to her. 'Where's Anna?'

'I thought you were leaving.' Rosa stared at her sister's ex with loathing. Hadn't he told Anna he'd be leaving the island the minute the speeches were over? If he had nothing more to offer, then as far as Rosa was concerned, the sooner he left, the better.

'I need to speak to Anna.'

'Maybe she doesn't want to speak to you.' And even if she did, maybe she shouldn't.

'Maybe,' Leo acknowledged. 'It's important, Rosa, please.'

Rosa sat staring at the stage, at Jude. She didn't want Anna to have to wait three years for closure, as they had. 'She'll be back at the villa. She's overseeing the clean-up and packing.'

'Packing?'

'She's heading back to Oxford tomorrow.' Leaving Rosa to manage the week of post-wedding festivities Valentina had requested. Yay. Except, right now, Rosa couldn't deny her sister anything. Not if it meant Anna finally finding the life she wanted.

'I thought she was staying here?' Leo sounded surprised.

'Mama wants her to go back and think about it. It's a huge change. Everyone just wants her to be sure. To make sure she's doing it for the right reasons.' She gave him a sidelong glance.

'Thanks.' Leo got to his feet.

Rosa tried to resist the urge to say anything more, and failed.

'Leo? She's actually doing really well. If you are going to make matters worse then stay away or I'll make you sorry you ever messed with my sister.' Threat made, she turned her attention back to the stage, clearly dismissing him.

'Warning understood,' Leo said and walked away.

'It better be,' Rosa muttered, under her breath. But then Jude, still up on stage, started speaking, and she forgot all about her sister's problems for a moment.

'This is my last song tonight,' Jude said, to a chorus of groans and calls for more. He held up a hand. 'No, really. But I just wanted to say, before I play it, that I wrote this one here, on La Isla Marina. I think this island has romance woven into its soil and stone and sand, because I've never felt as inspired as I do here. Although, that might be down to a certain muse re-entering my life, too.' He looked straight at Rosa as he said it, and her heart stuttered at everything she saw in his eyes. 'I'll be leaving the island soon, but I know my memories of this place will live on. And, Valentina, Todd… if your marriage is half as happy as I've been here on the island, you'll be very fortunate indeed. And I hope that it's twice as happy as that. So, this one is for the bride and groom.'

But it wasn't, Rosa realised as he started to pluck the strings, in the traditional Spanish style. It was *her* song. The one he'd written for her as she'd lain naked in his bed the night before.

She watched his face as he sang, saw all the emotion that was bursting to escape from her heart echoed there. And as his bright blue gaze met hers as he sang of water on skin and moon-light overhead, a bone-deep truth resounded through her.

She was in love with Jude Alexander.

And there was nothing she could do about it, because he was going to leave her, this time.

For good.

The week that followed the wedding had been planned as five days of non-stop entertainment for the wedding guests. Since Anna had left for Oxford (with Leo in tow, after what must have been a lot of grovelling on Leo's part, Jude imagined) Rosa was in charge, which meant she was rather busier than Jude would have liked. Given that it was their last week on the island together, he'd have preferred she had nothing to concentrate on but him, but apparently that wasn't how this worked.

'Sorry,' she'd murmur against his skin as she slipped out of his bed in the morning. 'There's cookery lessons at the villa today.' Or, 'I'm tak-ing a group horse-riding over on the mainland.'

'Can't you skive off, just for one day?' he'd asked, on the second morning. 'Stay here with me. We can go skinny-dipping again. Or you could finally show me the secret door to your bedroom…'

'Sorry,' she'd said again, smiling sadly. 'Anna left me in charge. And for once, I'm actually trying to live up to my obligations.'

And how was he supposed to argue with that?

There were a few trips he joined in with, though—namely the tapas tour of Cala del Mar, and the wine tasting at a local vineyard on the mainland. Rosa was too busy to dedicate all her time to him on those trips, but just the shared smiles across the room or a moment enjoying a plate of *gambas* together was enough to keep him going until the evening.

And the evenings, once all the entertainment was over, were magical.

It was as if, with their limited time together shrinking by the hour, they'd both been possessed with a sense of urgency that outshone even their previous passion. Jude didn't know how Rosa was coping on so little sleep, but she never seemed tired when she arrived at his bungalow in the evening. They'd fall asleep in each other's arms hours later, and then, before he knew it, Rosa would be slipping away, murmuring her apologies.

The coldness she left behind only made him more intent on enjoying every last second they had together.

But if their nights brought them closer than ever, the days seemed to put a strange barrier between them. He was a guest, no longer helping Rosa with the arrangements, but dancing attendance on Valentina and the others instead. Just being surrounded by the sort of people he was used to partying with in New York made him feel hemmed in again, and he seemed to spend his time dodging conversations about life in the city, or his plans for after the week was up. Most of all, he seemed to be avoiding Sylvie, who never had been very good at reading when a person didn't want to spend time with her.

Rosa, of course, charmed everyone she spoke to. She swept through the events and the days with a smile and a ready hand, fixing whatever needed fixing, keeping everything running so smoothly even Anna would be proud of her, Jude thought. But he was sure the only reason her easy charm never failed was because she knew this was only temporary. Five days of making nice with celebrities and rich folk and she'd be back to her real life.

Except this *was* his real life, to a point. He would be going back to this soon enough.

Was it so wrong of him to want to spend his last few days on the island with Rosa?

But she had work to do, so he let her get on

with it, smiling at her across rooms and waiting for night to fall so she could be just his again.

For their last night on the island, Rosa had arranged a moonlight picnic on the beach for everyone. Given how late the sun set, quite apart from his objections to spending his last evening with Rosa with a crowd of people, Jude thought this was kind of stupid, but Valentina had assured him it was romantic.

'You should definitely come,' she'd said, with a sly smile. 'You need more romance in your life.'

'I have plenty of romance,' Jude had replied, thinking of Rosa naked in his arms.

Valentina, seemingly reading his mind, had slapped his arm. 'That's not romance, Jude. Come on, join us tonight. And bring your guitar.'

'Now the truth comes out. I knew you only wanted me for my music.'

Valentina had laughed. 'I think Rosa and Todd would object to me wanting anything more, don't you?'

So that was how he came to be playing all the usual songs in an unusual place, sitting on a piece of driftwood on the beach, watching the moon play on the water. They'd lit a bonfire a little way away, and the staff were providing marshmallows and sticks to toast them on. They also had a full barbecue set up a little further away, as well as the picnic buffet. By the look of the amount of food and alcohol laid on, they were expecting this thing to go on all night. In which case there'd be a lot of hungover guests staggering to the boats to catch their flights home tomorrow.

Maybe he and Rosa could escape early, though, once everyone was suitably sloshed.

At least it wasn't the same beach where he and Rosa had gone for their fateful swim. He wasn't sure he'd have been able to keep his mind on the music if his brain had been reliving that night over and over. As it was, it was hard not to remember Rosa emerging from the sea, naked and glistening like a water goddess.

A discordant twanging sound came from his guitar, and he realised he'd managed to break a string, just imagining Rosa naked. Thankfully, everyone was so busy talking, eating and drinking no one was even paying all that much attention to his playing, so he retrieved a spare string from his case and set about restringing the instrument.

'You okay there?' Rosa sank to the sand in front of him, her legs folded under her, as he finished fixing his guitar. Her eyes shone in the firelight, her dark hair curling loose over her shoulders for once, just as it was in bed at night.

'Depends,' he said, tuning up. 'Do you think we can get out of here soon?'

Rosa gave him a cheeky grin. 'You're just never going to see the ocean the same way again, are you?'

'Apparently not.' No point denying what he'd been thinking about. Not with Rosa. Especially since he was almost certain she'd been thinking the same.

'Play me my song again,' she said, softly. 'One more time, and then I'll take you to bed.'

'Your wish is my command,' Jude said, and started to play.

They only had one more night together. He'd give her anything she asked.

CHAPTER TWELVE

THE FAMILIAR NOTES rose up into the night, circling above the fire, the beach, the crowd, the sea. Rosa closed her eyes and let them wash over her. She couldn't look at Jude as he played, even less so when he sang. The words cut too close, piercing her chest and brushing up against her heart.

She'd spent so long keeping everything away from there, ensuring that no one could lasso her heart and use it to keep her tied down. But it seemed that Jude had snuck in there against her best defences, anyway.

She was in love with Jude Alexander. She'd hoped that sudden truth of feeling might pass, but the week since the wedding had only confirmed it for her. She'd spent her days running events for the wedding guests, her brain only half functioning—because the other half was still thinking about Jude. And her nights... nothing about her nights with him had gone any way at all to persuading her to fall *out* of love with him.

The worst part was, she was starting to think nothing would.

She was irrevocably in love with Jude Alexander, and it was entirely possible she had been for the last three years and was only now coming out of denial.

She'd tried to tell herself that it didn't matter. It didn't change anything. Their situations were still exactly as they had been, so what difference did her feelings make? She'd vowed to make the most of their last week together, and then she'd move on. Just as she had a hundred times before. Easy.

But now she was down to counting in hours, and he was singing her song, and nothing about it felt easy at all.

How had she let this happen? She'd been so careful, always, not to let anything trap her with obligations and expectations. She'd rebelled against her father's academic expectations, lived down to Anna's expectations for her family life, run away from Jude's hopes for love and a future for them...and she'd ended up here, anyway.

Maybe Jude was right. Maybe them both being on the island at the same time was fate, or destiny. A way of making them face up to their demons.

But when her demons were as good-looking as Jude, it was so damn hard not to be tempted by them.

'I'll always see you in the moonlight,' Jude sang, the song coming to a close with a few more notes, and when Rosa opened her eyes he was staring right down into them.

She could stay lost in those blue eyes for eternity. And that terrified her almost as much as it excited her.

'Let's go,' she whispered. 'Now.'

Jude's slow smile was all the agreement she needed.

Rosa's body thrummed with anticipation as they slipped away from the beach, treading the familiar path back to Jude's bungalow. But for once, it wasn't the expectation of his hands on her body that made her blood buzz. This was something entirely new.

This wasn't sex. This was love.

Because she had to tell him. She couldn't let him leave without knowing how she felt.

Maybe it would change nothing, but she knew she'd never forgive herself if she didn't try. And as her family well knew, Rosa didn't know how to *not* say whatever was on her mind.

The moment the bungalow door closed behind them, Jude dropped his guitar case to the floor and his hands were at her waist, his mouth at her neck, and it took all her mental strength to say, 'Wait.'

If they started this, she wouldn't be able to stop it. And they needed to talk first.

Jude pulled back, just enough to look into her eyes. 'What's the matter?' The concern in his voice was a warm comfort around her heart.

He'd loved her once. Maybe he could again.

Maybe even enough to give her what she needed to be able to have this.

'I need to…can we talk? Just for a moment?'

If he said no, this wouldn't last any longer, anyway. And if he said yes…then there was no rush any more. They could take all the time in the world.

The expanse of for ever stretching out before them, together, for the first time didn't feel like a life sentence. Like a punishment.

It felt like the ultimate in opportunity.

As long as it could happen her way.

'Sure.' Frowning, Jude led her to the small seating area, pouring them each a glass of wine from the carafe on the counter. 'What is it?'

Rosa bit her lip. She wasn't good at subtle; she never had been. And she couldn't twist words and make a fancy argument as Anna could. She relied on her pictures, an image to tell a hundred stories, with just a few words where necessary to illuminate the subject.

She wasn't a poet, like Jude. She couldn't express her emotions in clever rhyme and melody.

All she had was her truths.

What she knew to be true. So she started there.

'You need to leave New York.' Okay, so it wasn't the most romantic opening, but it was true.

Jude looked taken aback. 'Okay…why, exactly?'

'Because it's dragging you down. Your guilt for Gareth, your promises…and that place. When I met you three years ago, you were full of music, of life. And now…now it's all about the brand and the label and negotiations with the rest of the band and…don't you want to be free of that?'

'Maybe.' Jude put his glass down on the counter. 'But I owe it to Gareth's memory—'

'No! No, you don't.' That was what was keeping him back. The memory of a friend who couldn't ever be satisfied when he was alive, let alone now he was dead.

'You don't understand,' Jude started, but Rosa interrupted him again.

'Yes, I do. I understand that you made Gareth a promise to keep him alive. But you couldn't save him. No one could. It wasn't me being there, or even me leaving that made you break that promise. Gareth was an addict. He was sick, and he needed more help than one best friend saying, "That's a bad idea." And he needed to want that help. He needed to seek it out and find a way to break that addiction and he didn't. If he'd been ready to be helped, it wouldn't matter what was going on in your life. And even then…you couldn't give up your life to save his. He wouldn't want that, and you know it.' She felt breathless, saying all the words she knew he needed to hear but wouldn't want to.

'Maybe,' he acknowledged. 'But even if you're right, I still owe him. I made another promise, when he died, remember?'

'And you've fulfilled it! You found the fame you swore you'd both fight for. You've lived his success for him.' When would he see that he'd done everything he could? It was time to live his own life, his own choices now.

But Jude looked away. 'It's not enough.'

'It'll never be enough.' Rosa grabbed his hand where he stood beside her, willing him to understand. 'Nothing ever was, for Gareth. Even now…when does it stop? When do you say, I've gone as far as I can go?'

'I don't know.'

'Because that point doesn't exist!' She'd seen it before. And he *had* to believe her. 'You'll keep living your life for someone else—someone who isn't even here to see it—for ever. And you'll never be happy. And he'll never be satisfied.'

Jude shook his head, and Rosa knew he wasn't hearing her. 'It's not just about Gareth's memory, anyway. I also want to keep having a career, you know. Music was my life long before you came into it.'

'You'll always have that,' Rosa replied. 'Your music is iconic now. You could write advertising jingles for the rest of your life and it wouldn't take away from what you'd already accomplished.'

'Thanks for that vote of confidence in my musical future,' Jude said, drily.

Rosa waved a hand vaguely. 'You know what I mean.'

'I really don't.' His eyes serious, Jude moved to sit opposite her. 'Rosa. What, exactly, are you asking me to do?'

This was it. This was her last chance to put everything out on the line, and have him take it or leave it.

Take her or leave her.

And Rosa had never been more scared in her life.

She took a deep breath.

'Run away with me.'

* * *

Run away with me.

How many times over the years had he dreamt of hearing that from her? Of knowing Rosa wanted him with her, as she explored this wide world? Of having her choose him, for once, over her freedom?

Except she wasn't, was she? That was what it came down to.

She wasn't ready to give up what they had, but she wouldn't give up anything else, either.

Rosa didn't just want to have her cake and eat it, too. She wanted the damn bakery to deliver.

'You want me to give up everything I have—my band, my career, my life in New York, my future—to travel around the world at your beck and call until you get bored of me again?' Anger rose up in him, hot and furious, as he realised the truth of this.

This wasn't love. This wasn't for ever—because they both knew Rosa couldn't offer that. She never had been able to.

This was convenience. It was using his unsettled feelings, his vulnerabilities after the book's release, after Gareth, to get what she wanted.

If she'd approached it differently—suggested he extend his sabbatical away from the city until the buzz about the book died down—maybe he'd have considered it. But it was always all or nothing with Rosa. No compromise, no middle path. She didn't know how, and she wasn't willing to learn.

He looked down into her wide, dark eyes, and realised the truth.

He loved her. Of course he did. But that simply wasn't going to be enough.

'That's not what I was saying,' Rosa started.

Jude shook his head. 'Yes. It is.'

'No! Jude... I—'

'Don't say it.' If she was even *thinking* what he thought she was about to say, he couldn't hear it. He couldn't risk it. If she told him she loved him, there was no way he could walk away again, not knowing that. He'd give up everything to trail her around the world, and he'd end up resenting her for it.

A shocked laugh bubbled up from somewhere inside him.

'What's so funny?' Rosa asked, scowling.

'I just realised,' Jude said. 'This must be exactly how you felt, three years ago.' How Sancia felt in Oxford with the professor. How Gareth felt sometimes when Jude kept him safe, back at the hotel instead of out at the party where he wanted to be, blazing bright.

Maybe Rosa was right. Maybe he never could have saved Gareth. But he could decide to save himself from any more heartbreak.

It wasn't much. But it was what he had left.

'So you're punishing me. Is that it?' Rosa jumped to her feet, her colour high and her eyes blazing. 'I left you three years ago, so you won't even consider staying now? I know I hurt you, but, Jude, this is just petty.'

'Petty! Rosa, you tore my heart out and stamped on it, then breezed back into my life and told me you'd just been ready for something new!'

'I explained—' Rosa started, but Jude was in no mood to hear it. All he'd wanted was one last night with Rosa, one perfect memory to say goodbye on.

Instead he got this. Everything he ever wanted on a plate, except he knew it was laced with poison.

'You explained. Right. But what it came down to was the same thing it will always come down to with you. You value your own freedom, your own choices, above everyone else's. And that might work for you with the rest of the world. But for the people who love you? It's horrible.'

The colour faded from Rosa's face as she stumbled backwards, grabbing a chair for support. 'What do you mean? Is it so wrong for me to want to pursue my own dreams?'

'No,' Jude allowed. 'But is it wrong of me to want to stay and look for my own?' New York might not be everything he'd ever dreamed of, but he knew the rules there. He knew he was as safe as it was possible to get, knew he could look himself in the mirror and know he was living out his promise. New York had always been their dream—and Rosa was asking him to give it up.

'But you're not!' Frustration leaked out of Rosa's voice. 'You're doing what the label says you should, or the rest of the band. You're not making new music, you're just remaking the old stuff! Living for a memory. Does fame really mean so much to you that you can't give it up to pursue the music that really makes you come alive again? Like the song you wrote here, for me?'

Did she really not see? Did she really not understand? One look at her face told Jude she didn't.

'That wasn't the music, Rosa. That was you.'

'What?'

Scrubbing a hand through his hair, Jude sighed. 'I wrote that song—found the passion and the music—because I found you again. For three years, it didn't much matter what I wrote or played because you weren't there to hear it.'

'Then why didn't you come after me?' From the way her eyes widened, and her hand went to her mouth, Rosa was as shocked by her words as he was.

'How could I? You didn't tell me where you were going.'

'And in this day and age, with the Internet and everything, there was absolutely no way you could find out?' She was right, Jude knew. He *could* have found her if he'd wanted to.

But he hadn't.

'Gareth had just died. Forgive me if—' But she could always tell when he was lying.

'That's not why, is it? Tell me the truth, Jude. We owe each other that much.'

'I didn't come after you because I knew I couldn't take it if you turned me away again. You knew me, Rosa. You knew every depth of me, more than any other person in the world. And you turned your back on it and walked away. No, I didn't come after you. Because I loved you, and I knew I could never, ever be enough for you.'

'But you are!' Rosa surged forward, grabbing his hands to her chest. 'You are. You're everything I need. That's why I'm here, asking you. Come with me! I don't see what the problem is. We can run together, keep having the same fun we've been having here on the island. It doesn't have to end yet.'

'Yet.' That was what it came down to, wasn't

it? With Rosa, there was always a time limit—
and only she knew what that might be. And Jude
couldn't live like that.

He'd known, deep down, that Gareth had a
time limit, too. That however hard he tried, Gareth lived too hard, too fast, to live for ever, or
even to old age. He just hadn't expected it to
be so soon. He'd thought he could buy more
time—just as he'd tried to do again on the island with Rosa.

God, he was an idiot. Trying to control time,
and other people. Both were equally impossible.

The only thing he could control was himself.
He could keep *himself* safe, even if he couldn't
ever have done the same for Gareth.

Rosa would leave, sooner or later. It was all
there in that tiny three-letter word: *yet*.

Rosa stilled as she finally caught his meaning. 'Nothing lasts for ever, Jude. Can't we just
enjoy this while it *does* last?'

Jude shook his head.

'Why not?' Rosa slammed her hand down on
the counter. 'Jude, I love you. Whether you want
to hear it or not. And right now, I can't imagine ever loving another person my whole life—
I haven't before, and I can't see that changing.'

The words pierced him straight through his
body. She loved him. This was what he had always wanted.

And he was going to send it away. His choice, this time.

'So you'd marry me? Promise me for ever? Go with me wherever life took me?'

He didn't need to hear her answer. He could see it in the fear on her face.

'Why couldn't you come wherever I went?' she asked.

'Because I won't give up everything I have when I know that one day—sooner or later—you'll walk out on me again,' he said, simply. 'It almost broke me last time, Rosa. I can't risk it twice.'

'You can't trust me.'

'Can you tell me I should?'

She looked away. 'No.'

'Then I don't think there's anything more to say. Do you?'

She didn't answer.

Grabbing his guitar, Jude walked out on the love of his life.

He didn't look back.

CHAPTER THIRTEEN

TEARS BLINDED HER as Rosa raced up the path back to the villa. Thank goodness everyone was leaving tomorrow. She could be packed and on a boat with them first thing, and on a plane to Russia, or Australia—anywhere—before breakfast. She needed to get as far away from La Isla Marina, and Jude Alexander, as possible—and fast.

What had she been thinking? Of course he wouldn't give up all his successes and fame to run away with her. Who would? Rosa had always been the screw-up, the wild and free one who couldn't settle for anything. Now it seemed she couldn't live up to Jude's expectations any more than she'd lived up to her father's or her sister's. She couldn't live up to his life in New York, or the memory of the best friend he'd lost. Especially when she couldn't promise him for ever.

Except…she'd wanted to. For a heartbeat of

a moment, when he'd asked if she'd marry him, she'd wanted to say yes. Wanted to fall into his arms and be his for ever.

Until he'd added 'go with me' and she'd known she couldn't promise that.

She wasn't a follower. And neither was Jude. Neither of them would ever be happy trailing around after the other.

It was an impossibility. *They* were an impossibility.

It had been fun while it lasted, but she should never have expected anything more. She wasn't good at compromise, or giving, or other people's feelings. Hadn't Anna made that clear enough?

Her sister could change her path, change her mind, her life. But Rosa never had been able to live up to Anna's example.

For one, sharp moment Rosa missed her sister so much that it ached. They might not have always—okay, often—got along, but Anna was still family. She'd turned to Rosa when she'd found out she was pregnant, eventually, and now Rosa wished that she could do the same.

But Anna was far away in Oxford with Leo, and all Rosa had left were her parents. The mother who'd taught her that the best way to deal with difficulties was to run away, and the father who'd always wanted her to be someone she wasn't.

Somehow, she couldn't see either of them fixing this mess.

Wiping her tears away, Rosa stepped into the main villa, the place she'd spent so many childhood holidays, that held so many memories.

Then she stopped.

And she stared.

'Mama?' she whispered. Sancia didn't hear her. *'Dad?'* Louder this time. 'What are you doing?'

Sancia and Ernest broke apart, and Rosa regretted her question. It was pretty obvious what they were doing.

Kissing.

Her parents.

After ten years apart. Estranged. Not speaking. Now suddenly they were…

Kissing. Passionately.

'Rosa!' Sancia patted her hair as she smiled at her daughter. 'Um, we have some news!'

'So I can see.' Rosa crossed her arms over her chest. Was *everyone* else finding their happy ever after on this island? Or, more likely, was this sudden reconciliation going to end in disaster—just as Jude and hers had?

Sancia's brow furrowed. 'Are you okay, *querida*? Did something happen?'

'I just caught my parents making out. Other

than that…' She didn't want anyone to know about Jude. Not yet.

Not when his words still hurt so much.

Her father pulled a face. 'Making out? Really, Rosa. Is it so wrong for two people in love to express their affection for each other?'

'When they're *my* parents…' Rosa shook her head. 'Never mind. Just…what's going on? What's your news?' In love? Had she really heard those words from her buttoned-up father's mouth?

'Your father is moving here to the island!' Sancia practically vibrated with excitement.

Rosa blinked. And she'd thought Anna's decision to stay on La Isla Marina was the about-turn of the century.

'Here? You're staying here?' she asked her father.

Ernest put his arm around Sancia and nodded. 'I think it's about time. Don't you?'

Time? Was that all it took? If she waited another decade would she be able to make things work with Jude? Somehow, she doubted he'd be willing to wait that long.

'But…how can you just give up everything you've worked for in Oxford? All your old dreams?' His career at the university, his professional reputation—they'd been all that mattered to him, when she was growing up. Everything in their lives had been arranged around them. And now he was just throwing them away? It didn't make any sense.

'Your mother needs support here on the island. And Anna will be here, too, so I'd be alone in Oxford.'

So that was it. Of course. 'You mean, your nursemaid is moving here so you better had, too?'

'No.' Ernest's voice was sharp. 'I'm moving here for many reasons. Not least, my health and well-being. Rosa, you've told me often enough over the years that I need to take responsibility for my health. I'd think you'd be glad I'm finally retiring to do that.'

'I am,' Rosa said, quickly. 'I just...'

Sancia pulled away to put an arm around Rosa's shoulders. 'What is it, *querida*?'

Rosa looked at her mother. 'Ten years ago you got fed up of living the life Dad wanted all the time, and you left to come here. To find your own dreams again. Right?'

'I suppose,' Sancia said. 'I was tired of always coming second to his work and not being able to follow my heart. But most of all, I just missed my home, and my parents needed me more than he did.' Her smile turned sad. 'Even more than you girls did, in some ways. Your father and I were arguing more and more, and it was making me so unhappy… I knew it had to be affecting you and Anna, too. I didn't want you to grow up in an unhappy home, and I didn't want to regret staying when I should have gone…but, Rosa, leaving you girls behind, only seeing you in the holidays, that was the hardest choice I ever had to make. You know that, don't you?'

'I do,' Rosa said as Sancia hugged her close. Her mother had always made it clear that her leaving was nothing to do with the girls—even if it had taken Rosa a while to believe it when she was younger.

Perhaps that was why she'd never asked her mother outright for all the reasons she'd left. She'd listened to what Sancia said, tried to believe it, and always just assumed it was because she was tired of life in Oxford.

But now she needed firm answers. She needed to understand. 'Dad, what if the same thing happens to you?'

'What do you mean?' Ernest asked.

'What if, living here, you get, well, bored? You're giving up everything that has always mattered to you. I don't want you to end up resenting Mama for that in a few months, or years. When you realise you're tied to her dreams and obligated to stay.'

She'd never seen the smile on her father's

face before, Rosa realised. It was softer, kinder, more indulgent than any smile he'd given her before.

Professor Gray held a hand out to Sancia, who took it with a smile of her own. Rosa watched, confused.

'You're forgetting my most important reason to stay here, Rosa,' her father said. 'I'm in love with your mother.'

Love. The word caught her in the throat. Did it always have to come down to that?

'What if that isn't enough?' she asked, and the concern on Sancia's face returned.

'Rosa, did something happen with Jude?' she asked.

'I just need to know,' Rosa said desperately, her arms wrapped tight around her middle. 'What if love isn't enough?'

'Then nothing is,' Sancia said, simply.

'When it's true love, staying isn't an obligation. It's a privilege.' Professor Gray pressed a kiss to his ex-wife's head. 'I'm giving up my old dreams for new ones. Better ones.'

'We got it wrong last time,' Sancia said. 'Both of us. We thought there were more important things than love.'

'Aren't there?' Rosa felt as if the bottom were falling out of her heart.

'There are things that matter as much,' Professor Gray allowed. 'And there are circumstances that can overwhelm it, if you're not careful.'

'So if it's love, you have to give up everything?' Because that didn't sound like love to her.

'No, *querida*.' Sancia moved forward, guiding Rosa with an arm around her shoulder to one of the low, cushioned benches that were scattered around the reception area. 'Love is about accepting the other person as they are, and loving them in spite of your differences.'

'Or because of them,' her father added, sitting down beside her. 'Your mother and I... we're very different people. But those differences don't lessen our love any.'

'And in some ways they even make us stronger,' Sancia added. 'As long as we accept them and respect them.'

'You mean he has to love me for who I am?' Because in that case, there really was no hope for Jude and her.

Sancia laughed, lightly. 'That's the easy part, *querieda*. Who could not love you?'

Rosa stared at her mother in amazement. 'You *have* to love me. You're my parents. But I know I'm not easy to love. I know it's in spite of all my flaws and not because of them. I'm no Anna.'

'We never wanted you to be Anna,' Sancia said, surprised. 'We just wanted you to be happy.'

Beside her, Rosa's father was nodding his agreement. Rosa looked at him in confusion. 'But… I never could follow the schedule or plan ahead. I couldn't settle to anything, especially not studying.'

'And none of that meant we loved you any less,' Ernest said. 'Or that we were any the less proud of you than we are of Anna.'

Rosa blinked, tears burning behind her eyes again.

'Oh, Rosa.' Sancia hugged her tightly. 'How could you think you are difficult to love? You're so full of life and spirit.'

'Just like your mother. That's one of the many reasons I fell in love with her,' Ernest put in. 'And you've taken that spirit out into the world, forging your own, brilliant path. Your sister collects all your photos and articles and saves them for me, you know. I have them all catalogued in my office.' He said it so casually, as if it were obvious. An inevitability. But the knowledge lifted Rosa's heart, even in the middle of her misery.

'We're very proud of you, *querida*,' Sancia said. 'And we love you very much. And if Jude doesn't, then he's a fool.'

Rosa shook her head. 'He's not. Last time… I left him. I broke his heart.'

'I wonder where you learnt to do that,' Ernest murmured, but he was smiling fondly at Sancia as he said it.

'Then he's a coward, if he won't take the risk of loving you again.' Sancia looked outraged on Rosa's behalf.

'I don't blame him,' Rosa admitted. 'I'm not sure I would. I'm asking him to give up everything.'

'Love does take some compromise, Rosa,' her father said, gently. 'But the rewards should always be greater than whatever you have to give up.'

'In the end, love is the only thing that lasts,' Sancia said, smiling at her husband as she stood, holding her hand out to him. 'And it's worth ten times of everything else.'

'Which is why we won't make the same mistakes again.' Rosa's father got to his feet, too, taking Sancia's hand.

'I'm glad,' Rosa said, the words thick in her throat. 'I'm glad you found each other again.'

'So am I,' Sancia said, and then Ernest swept her into his arms again, and Rosa turned away.

She couldn't watch their happiness. Not tonight.

Tomorrow. Tomorrow she'd be happy for them.

She'd smile and offer congratulations on her way off the island.

Tonight, she just needed to mourn her own broken heart, and think about all the compromises she hadn't been willing to make, until it was too late.

And then she'd move on.

Jude didn't trust her love. She hadn't left herself any other choices.

Jude hadn't exactly planned on heading back to the beach, but that was where he found himself, all the same.

The party was winding down, the fire burning down low. Couples were dotted around the sand in cosy embraces, talking low, and Valentina and Todd were dancing on the shoreline as if there were no one else in the world but them.

Jude looked away. He couldn't quite bear to watch that kind of happiness tonight.

Settling back onto his piece of driftwood, he pulled his guitar from its case again. Music had always been his friend, his comfort, and he needed it tonight more than ever, since the day he lost Gareth.

Rosa would be leaving as soon as she could, of course. And he'd be left behind again, with his heart in tatters. Meeting Rosa had torn his life apart the first time, but he'd honestly thought he could withstand it this time. How much worse could she do to him, after all?

It turned out, quite a lot.

She loved him. Or she thought she did. Just not enough to give up any iota of her freedom, or give him any hope that she wouldn't leave him again without a backward glance.

Rosa was right, of course. Nothing did last for ever, and there were no guarantees in this life. Gareth had taught him that.

But he needed more than she could give him. He needed...something. Some sign that she was in this as deeply as he was. That she wanted it to last as much as he did.

Was that too much to ask?

'I didn't expect to see you back here tonight.' Sylvie settled herself onto the sand in front of him, too close to where Rosa had sat for Jude to feel comfortable with it.

'You know me. Always the last at a party.'

'Yes,' Sylvie allowed. 'But that was usually because I didn't want to leave until everyone else who mattered had. You never cared for them for yourself.'

'I'll have to get used to them again, I suppose,' Jude said.

'You're definitely coming back to New York, then?' Sylvie sounded surprised. 'I know Rosa said you were, but I assumed she was just being careful. That she was hoping you'd go with her, but she didn't want to fall too deep in case you didn't feel the same. It's what I would do.'

Jude gave a low laugh. 'Trust me, Rosa is never careful. With anything.' Including his heart.

'That's why you love her, I suppose,' Sylvie said, her head tilted to her shoulder as she looked up at him. 'She's so free and open. Like you were, when you first came to the city.'

'Who said I loved her?'

Sylvie's smile was sad. 'Oh, Jude. Anyone who has seen you together this week knows that. You're not subtle, my dear.'

'I wasn't trying to be.' He hadn't been trying to be anything, here. Not a celebrity, not a star. Not a musician. Not Gareth's best friend. Not even Jude Alexander, brand.

He hadn't even tried to be enough for Rosa— he'd known there wasn't any point.

He'd been just Jude. Himself.

And Rosa had loved him. Not enough to stay, sure, but enough to tell him. For Rosa, that was a lot.

More than he'd have expected, before tonight.

'It's better this way.' Sylvie stretched her long legs out over the sand. 'I know you don't love me. I'm not sure if I love you either, to be honest. But I think love might be overrated. You don't need love—especially not if it makes you look as miserable as you do tonight.'

'What do I need, then?' Jude asked, honestly curious. Maybe there was another path. One that hurt less. That would be good.

'You need someone to look pretty next to you at awards ceremonies. Someone who doesn't object to you being away on tour for half the year, or mind when you lock yourself away to write for days on end. Someone to keep the groupies and whackos at bay, at least a little bit. Someone who gets as much from the association as you do. Someone who fits your level of stardom.'

'Someone like you?' he guessed.

'Why not?' Sylvie shrugged those elegant shoulders. 'We were good together, Jude, admit it. It might not be love, but it was enough. Satisfactory satisfaction, if you like.'

She was right, Jude realised. Sylvie had been the picture-perfect partner for him, supporting his brand, making sure he was seen at the right places, giving him—and the band—the right level of glamour. Gareth would have been jealous as all hell.

No, Gareth would have snagged Sylvie himself, and shown her off all over the world. Gareth would have lived the life Jude had now with style and flourish and excitement. He'd have loved it.

But the thought of going back to it made Jude feel as if the sea were closing in over his head and taking him down.

And Rosa was the only one that could save him, pull him out of the water he'd been treading for too long.

'I can't do it, Sylvie.' He shook his head, placing his guitar back in its case, as clarity flowed over him like the tide. 'I can't live like that again.'

Rosa was right. Well, no, she was still more wrong than right about a lot of things. But she was right about him.

He had to let Gareth's memories, the broken promises, and all the expectations go.

He needed to be free every bit as much as she did.

And the only time he ever felt free to be himself was when he was with Rosa.

Which only left him with one option.

She couldn't promise him anything, but then nobody could. Not really. He knew, better than anyone, that some promises just weren't possible to keep.

Maybe they didn't need any promises. Maybe all they needed was love.

And the willingness to risk everything for it. Because some people were worth the risk. One person, anyway.

Gareth would have. Gareth always believed a risk was worth it, if the prize was big enough. For Gareth, the prize was always fame.

For Jude, it was Rosa.

And suddenly, Jude knew he would risk it, too.

CHAPTER FOURTEEN

ROSA'S TURRET BEDROOM had always been an escape, before. A place of refuge from her family, or the guests on the island, or whatever. But now it felt like a cell, one she couldn't wait to escape.

She folded the yellow dress she'd worn for the wedding and placed it in her case, followed by the skirt she'd stripped off on the beach the night she went swimming with Jude. Tears dripped onto the fabric, and she shoved it in fast. She couldn't think about Jude. Possibly ever again, but definitely not until she'd put some considerable air miles between them.

She needed to move on. She didn't have any other choice now.

Maybe her parents were right and love could overcome, but not for her and Jude. She'd already burned that bridge. He was probably halfway off the island by now, and she wouldn't chase him. She smiled, sadly, remembering the reasons he'd given for not chasing her three years ago. Suddenly, she understood, in a way she couldn't have before. Not until she'd lived the same moment.

But things were different now. She understood herself better, and her relationship with her family. She was a different person. Maybe, in time, her dreams would shift, too. Maybe she'd even meet someone else, one day. In the distant, distant future. But even as she thought it, she couldn't believe it. Who could live up to Jude Alexander?

So, it was just her. Just like before. That was okay. She'd go to Russia. The story there sounded interesting, important. She'd get her camera out and seek truths through its lens. She'd live the life she'd always promised herself she'd have.

And she might not be happy, but she could be content. She could be herself. And that wasn't nothing.

But then the door to her room flew open and she spun to see Jude standing there, too big in the narrow doorway, his bright blue eyes wild and his black hair crazy.

Swallowing down the last of her tears, Rosa fought to keep her chin level and her voice even. It seemed absurd that, after everything they'd shared over the last few weeks, this was the first time he'd ever even been in her room. 'You found the secret door at last, then?'

'Your mother showed me.' His voice was rough, as if he was as close to tears as she was.

Damn Sancia. Wasn't her mama supposed to be on her side?

'What do you want, Jude?' Hadn't they said enough terrible, hurtful things to each other already? Rosa wasn't sure she could stand to hear any more.

But Jude looked her straight in the eye and said, 'You.'

'I think you made it very clear that you don't,' Rosa said, looking away. 'If you've come here to rub it in some more—'

'I haven't.' Jude stepped closer, taking the dress she was holding from her hands. 'Rosa, just listen? Please?'

It was the please that undid her. She never could deny him when he asked her in that voice. Why else had she had to disappear without word, last time? If he'd asked her to stay…she still wasn't sure she could have said no.

'Okay.'

She couldn't imagine what he'd have to say that could possibly make anything between them any better, though. He'd made it very clear that it was up to her to change the conversation—to change her mind, her direction.

Sancia had called him a coward. But it wasn't him, was it? *She* was the one who needed to be brave.

She needed to find the courage to make big promises. The for ever kind. And she might have to give up everything she'd ever fought for before to do that. Could she?

Would he even let her try?

Rosa thought again of the future she imagined—living her truths, being herself, being content. But never happy.

But what was her other option?

She had to make a promise she would have to keep. She had to live up to expectations for once, whatever her parents said.

She knew, deep down in her soul, that this was it for her.

This was love, and it was all she was going to get.

Anna had changed her dreams. Her life.

So had her father, and that had seemed impossible even a week ago.

Maybe she could do it, too.

She had to at least try, or she knew she'd regret it for the rest of her life.

'I've been thinking,' Jude said. 'I can't leave things as we did, not again. When you left me last time, I spent three years wondering what

I did wrong, wishing I could have one more chance to put it right.'

'Or for me to do it right,' Rosa put in, and he smiled.

'So this time, let's try, yeah?'

Hope bubbled up in her chest. 'You're giving me a second chance?' This was it. This time, she wouldn't screw it up. The third time was the charm, right? She just had to stamp down on all those impulses that told her to run. She could stay.

'I'm giving us as many chances as we need to get it right,' Jude said.

But Rosa wasn't listening. Her parents' words were echoing through her mind and finally, suddenly, it seemed possible. If she had Jude with her, she could do it all. Couldn't she?

'I've been thinking… I could come to New York. There's so many stories there, so many photos. I could work there. It could work.'

'Rosa.'

'I could stay in one place.'

'No, you couldn't.'

'I could come on tour with you, then.'

'And follow me round like a groupie?'

Why was he smiling? He kept shooting down every possibility she gave him, and he was doing it with a smile on his face.

'Jude…' She was begging. She was actually

going to beg. What the hell had he done to her? 'Just tell me what you need me to do and I'll do it. I'll do whatever it takes to be with you.'

Rosa's words stuck in his chest, and he caught her hands in his in their place, holding them to him. 'You don't understand. Rosa, you don't need to do anything. Except be you.'

She blinked up at him, those dark eyes he loved still wet with tears. Jude wanted to kiss away every tear on her cheek, but first he had to explain himself.

'I went back to the beach after you left. I spoke to Sylvie about New York and the more I imagined going back there, back to that same old life again...the more I knew I couldn't do it. I can't be that Jude Alexander any more. The man they wrote about in that book is gone—if he ever existed at all. And so is the best friend Gareth knew. I'm not the same, now. I can't play that part.'

'Well, I knew that,' Rosa muttered, and he smiled down at her.

'Yeah, well, you were always the expert at being true to yourself.'

'Even when it hurts others.'

'I shouldn't have said that,' Jude said.

Rosa gave a half shrug. 'It's true. I just... I don't know how to be anything else. But I'll learn. I'll figure it out if it means I get to be with you.'

'Luckily for both of us, I love you exactly the way you are,' Jude said, gratified by the sharp intake of breath his words caused in Rosa.

'You love me? Still?'

'Rosa, I've always loved you. From the moment you walked into my life three years ago, I always knew that there was no one else for me. No one else could be so full of life—or could make me feel so alive.' Jude took a breath. 'You asked me a question earlier, remember?' Rosa nodded. 'Will you ask me again?'

'Will you run away with me?' The hope in her eyes was what helped him answer. To step over the edge and give up the life he'd worked for, the fame, the proof that he was worth something, the dreams he and Gareth had dreamt together. Everything.

He'd risk everything for her.

'I'll run anywhere with you,' he said, and kissed her.

For a moment, the world seemed to tilt and turn and snap into place. For the first time in too many years, everything felt right. He didn't have to prove anything, any more. He didn't need to be anything except the man Rosa loved.

All he needed to do was love her back. And

it felt as if he'd already been doing that for ever, anyway.

Rosa broke the kiss. 'Wait. How is this going to work? What about the band?'

'I'll tell them I need a break. Or I'll take some time to write—and I can do that wherever you are.' He kissed her hands. 'I can't let you give up your dreams for me, but maybe neither of us needs to give up anything. Maybe we can both just chase them together.'

'Are you sure?'

'Surer than I've ever been about anything,' Jude said. 'Think about it. We can not settle down together. We can spend time in the city when I'm recording, perhaps, and maybe you'd like to come on tour sometimes, when you're not away working.'

'And the rest of the time?'

'I'll come with you. Wherever you want to go.'

'And we'll spend our summers on La Isla Marina with Anna and Leo and the baby, and Mama and Dad?'

'Of course,' Jude replied. 'One of these days I'm going to beat your father at Scrabble.'

'No,' Rosa said fondly. 'You're not. He cheats.'

'I knew it!'

'But you'll play him anyway?'

'I will. But only because it would be rude to refuse my wife's father a game.'

'Your wife?'

'You liked how I slipped that in there?' Jude asked, grinning.

'I know I'm unconventional about these things, but I seem to remember something about having to be asked, first.'

Jude dropped to one knee, her hands still tight in his as he looked up at her. 'Rosa Gray, will you chase your dreams with me?'

'Yes.'

'Will you love me for ever?'

'Definitely.'

'Will you let me love you and walk by your side for the rest of your life?'

'Oh, yes.'

'Then I think we might as well get married, don't you?'

Laughing, Rosa pulled him to his feet and kissed him, soundly. 'For a poet, that was incredibly unromantic.'

'I'll work on it,' Jude promised.

'Well, we do have for ever,' Rosa said, wrapping her arms around him. 'After all, I'm not going anywhere. At least, not without you.'

'That's all the promise I'll ever need from you,' Jude replied, and kissed her.

EPILOGUE

LA ISLA MARINA was beautiful in the late-afternoon sunlight. The tiny lights strung through the trees were already lit, glowing in the fading daylight, and lanterns lit the way to the pagoda, through the rows of chairs filled with friends and family, from the island, the mainland, Britain, the States and beyond.

Rosa peered around the corner, down to the pagoda where Jude already stood, her father at his side. Then her niece squirmed in her arms, and she resumed swaying in the way the baby seemed to like best, hoping she wasn't drooling on her dress. Being an auntie seemed to involve a lot of cuddles, which she was just fine with. Uncle Jude was better for the lullabies, though.

'Are you ready?' Rosa asked Sancia, as Anna fiddled with their mother's veil.

Sancia laughed. 'Ready? *Querida*, I've been ready for more than ten years. I was just waiting for your father to come to his senses and come after me.'

The fact that Sancia and Ernest had never actually got around to divorcing should have been a clue, Rosa thought. But at least it made things easier now—a vow renewal on the island was much more special than having to go to the mainland for a formal remarriage.

Anna held out her arms for her daughter, and Rosa handed her over, feeling a brief pang of emptiness as she did so.

It didn't last long, though. She pressed a hand to her stomach, and remembered that wherever she roamed now, she did it with company. First Jude, and, soon, their child.

Looking down at the path at her feet to hide her smile, Rosa thought how much this would have terrified her a few years ago. Not now, though.

Now, it all seemed like the biggest adventure she'd chased yet.

'Right, that's the first signal,' Anna said as the music changed. 'Everyone ready?'

They'd agreed that they'd walk their mother down the aisle together. It just felt right, since they were entrusting her to their father again. They both had their own lives to live now— Anna and Leo on the island, and Rosa and Jude wherever the mood took them.

Leo appeared to take the baby from Anna, and reclaim his seat at the front. Then Sancia linked arms with both her daughters, and they prepared to walk down the aisle, just as Anna had nine months earlier, still barely showing, to marry Leo. Jude and Rosa had managed to avoid the big showy wedding so far, and Rosa wasn't entirely looking forward to telling her mother that, technically, they were already married. She had a feeling that Sancia wouldn't feel the quick register office service when they were passing through London on tour would really count.

But it counted to Rosa.

Right until the moment she said yes, she'd been half afraid she'd run—and she knew Jude had, too. But when it came down to it, she knew that their love was far more binding than any piece of paper or jewellery.

Really, what more could she give Jude than her heart, anyway? And he'd had that all along.

'It's so wonderful to have both my girls together on the island again,' Sancia said, squeezing them close as they waited for that second change in the music, the one that told them it was time to start walking.

'It is nice to all be together,' Anna agreed.

'Rosa, will you come again for longer, later in the summer?'

'We'll try,' Rosa replied, as the music changed and Anna signalled for them to take their first steps. Rosa grinned as she saw Jude waiting with her father up ahead. 'But come winter we'll definitely be here for a few months,' she said, not thinking.

'Really?' Sancia stopped walking, a pace before the aisle started, and Rosa realised that the middle of her vow renewal service might not have been quite the right time to tell her mother this news.

Oh, well. Timing had never been her strong suit. Or not blurting things out the moment she thought of them.

'Why, Rosa?' Anna had a small line between her eyebrows.

Rosa shrugged. 'Well, I need you both to teach me everything you know about babies. And pretty fast.'

Sancia squealed, embracing her tightly, and Rosa saw her father rolling his eyes over her mother's shoulder.

'You made her smudge her make-up,' Anna said, with a sigh. But Rosa knew from the grin on her face that her sister was happy for her.

'Come on, Mama,' she said, disentangling herself. 'Dad's waiting.'

'Oh, he's waited this long,' Sancia said. 'A few more moments won't make a difference.'

'Besides,' Rosa agreed, smiling at Jude at the other end of the aisle, 'the best things in life are worth waiting for.'

* * * * *

If you missed the previous story in the **WEDDING ISLAND** *duet, look out for*

BABY SURPRISE FOR THE
SPANISH BILLIONAIRE
by Jessica Gilmore

And, if you enjoyed this story,
check out these other great reads
from Sophie Pembroke

NEWBORN UNDER THE
CHRISTMAS TREE
PROPOSAL FOR THE
WEDDING PLANNER
SLOW DANCE WITH THE BEST MAN
THE UNEXPECTED HOLIDAY GIFT

All available now!

Get 4 FREE REWARDS!

We'll send you 2 FREE Books <u>plus</u> 2 FREE Mystery Gifts.

FREE
Value Over
$20

Both the **Romance** and **Suspense** collections feature compelling novels written by many of today's best-selling authors.

YES! Please send me 2 FREE novels from the Essential Romance or Essential Suspense Collection and my 2 FREE gifts (gifts are worth about $10 retail). After receiving them, if I don't wish to receive any more books, I can return the shipping statement marked "cancel." If I don't cancel, I will receive 4 brand-new novels every month and be billed just $6.74 each in the U.S. or $7.24 each in Canada. That's a savings of at least 16% off the cover price. It's quite a bargain! Shipping and handling is just 50¢ per book in the U.S. and 75¢ per book in Canada*. I understand that accepting the 2 free books and gifts places me under no obligation to buy anything. I can always return a shipment and cancel at any time. The free books and gifts are mine to keep no matter what I decide.

Choose one: ☐ **Essential Romance**   ☐ **Essential Suspense**
                     (194/394 MDN GMY7)   (191/391 MDN GMY7)

Name (please print)

Address   Apt. #

City   State/Province   Zip/Postal Code

Mail to the **Reader Service**:
IN U.S.A.: P.O. Box 1341, Buffalo, NY 14240-8531
IN CANADA: P.O. Box 603, Fort Erie, Ontario L2A 5X3

Want to try two free books from another series! Call 1-800-873-8635 or visit www.ReaderService.com.

---

*Terms and prices subject to change without notice. Prices do not include applicable taxes. Sales tax applicable in NY. Canadian residents will be charged applicable taxes. Offer not valid in Quebec. This offer is limited to one order per household. Books received may not be as shown. Not valid for current subscribers to the Essential Romance or Essential Suspense Collection. All orders subject to approval. Credit or debit balances in a customer's account(s) may be offset by any other outstanding balance owed by or to the customer. Please allow 4 to 6 weeks for delivery. Offer available while quantities last.

Your Privacy—The Reader Service is committed to protecting your privacy. Our Privacy Policy is available online at www.ReaderService.com or upon request from the Reader Service. We make a portion of our mailing list available to reputable third parties that offer products we believe may interest you. If you prefer that we not exchange your name with third parties, or if you wish to clarify or modify your communication preferences, please visit us at www.ReaderService.com/consumerschoice or write to us at Reader Service Preference Service, P.O. Box 9062, Buffalo, NY 14240-9062. Include your complete name and address.

STRS18